THE CHARLATAN

Red Lamb

PRAV PUBLISHING

2025

PRAV Publishing
www.pravpublishing.com
prav@pravpublishing.com

ISBN 978-1-952671-71-5 (Paperback)
ISBN 978-1-952671-72-2 (Ebook)

THE CHARLATAN

1

Hell's Kitchen

"She's a blessed angel on earth; and after this one night I'll cling to her skirts and follow her to heaven."

— Nathaniel Hawthorne

Possessed by the spirits of drink, Jack Valentine found shelter in a gold-plated art-deco moviehouse off Ludlow, his respite from the infernal countdown to come. The picture was decent, something about technology and memory as a metaphor for drug addiction, set against a cyberpunk backdrop of charming rogues and brutal cops during the last forty-eight hours before the new millennium. A purist and a romantic, Jack didn't believe in escapist entertainment, preferring visual arts like Mississippi dip tobacco, material to chew on for a while then spit out, a light buzz of bliss and clarity circling his mental; however, in this particular instance the two-hour, twenty-million-dollar visitor from Hollywood projected on the big screen down in front provided literal escape from the demonic ritual soon to take place in every dive, club, hotel, and warehouse across the city. What appeared to be merely another day on the Gregorian calendar for the few served as a bizarre celebration for the many, an opportunity to worship time itself, a drunken scream of numbers reversed from ten in the name of Moloch.

Jack never understood the shine of this avoid-at-all-costs pseudo-event. His Turkish grade-school crush, a cheerleader with a prominent nose who barely knew his face, once told him that, in her culture, the friends and family surrounding you at the dawn of a new year's day were the ones you could expect to play pivotal roles during the following three hundred and sixty-five. Jack never understood that sentimental maxim, either. On the previous Dec. 31st, half a day after moving to New York City, he met a bisexual biker chick, with nipple piercings and no vaccine and a prominent nose, who rode him in reverse cowgirl 'til the sun rose over a leopard-print bedspread, then never spoke to him again.

The credits rolled and Jack embarked upstairs to the theater's commissary, an elegant homage to the studio cafeterias of historic Tinseltown. A cute imp of a hostess handed him a complimentary glass of bottom-shelf bubbly and wished him well. Jack's eyes locked onto the clock on the wall: fifteen minutes 'til midnight.

"Goddamnit."

The hostess glared at him and retracted her arm from the toasting position.

"Lord have mercy."

Jack retreated to an ornate couch and watched the proceedings alone, reminded of bygone feelings of alienation in clamorous social environments, a nightmarish fish-eye image of slack-jawed droolers endlessly remarking that "YOU GOTTA DO WHAT YOU GOTTA DO TO PAY THE RENT" while their companions laughed and laughed with tautological glee.

The digital interfaces silently switched to 11:59. The mass of revelers began revving their counting engines. Jack drained his cup of champagne and stumbled out into the night. He walked north through the East Village, toeing the line of demarcation between angry fraternity brothers and the aggressive homeless population, at war over control of the streets after dark.

Jack remembered that a retired stockbroker had invited him to a low-key meetup, for cinema enthusiasts and makers alike, which took place most Sunday evenings at a three-story bar named for the Russian secret service agency made infamous during the Cold War. He met Mr. Chang, the former trader, a couple months back at a lunch counter in Bushwick: Chinese owners, American slop, Chinese acquaintance, American man. After a touch of trouble with the federal government ignited a mild case of Surveillance Paranoia, Jack had swapped his clunky, little-used smartphone for a series of burner flips, failing to save the digits of fast friends. With no way to confirm his elder's presence at the spycraft-themed watering hole, he made his way blind to the joint off 2nd Avenue. Lining the walls were Bolshevik portraits, propaganda posters, cartoon drawings of animals in the house style of socialist realism, and the centerpiece: a flag with blue and yellow stripes dignifying the country of Ukraine, a figurative sign of the times, a totem to the current thing. Jack craned his head, searching for the elusive Mr. Chang before deciding to occupy an empty barstool near the corner.

"Where the fuck did you just blow in from?"

Jack glanced down at his chilly-weather outerwear—a stately cream duster with polka dots—then looked over at the bard who barked the rude remark: a public-domain jawbreaker, teal eyes set within the broad, flat head of a shark.

"Jack Valentine. I live here." He extended his palm.

"Since when? Yesterday?" The D-list bruiser licked a smirk off his lips and offered a large mitt to shake. "Stevie Delazzo, from the Bronx. I'm a painter, what's your IG?"

Jack signaled for the cruel Sapphic bartender.

"I quit all social media a couple years back. Communication and memory skills quickly improved. More fun in the real world." He ordered a tall glass of Japanese whiskey on ice. "Couldn't avoid a creeping sense of paranoia baked into every app and profile, not so much a feeling of being watched as one of subtle manipulation, my attention directed towards subjects most unsavory."

Stevie guzzled his beer, the fourth of its kind congregated on the bartop. "I hear you. I was up in Harlem last week to see my parole officer, and some little treadmark starts flapping his big mouth, asking me where I'm from, what I'm doing, who I'm here to see like he owns the fucking block, so I square my shoulders and say, 'Sup nigga? What's up?'

Kid goes scurrying off to his whore mother, thank God. I can't afford another assault rap, but respect on the street is fucking priceless. I would've beat his ass to dust. My ex-wife always nagged me the same way 'til I did the sensible thing and smacked her sideways. Of course the court sticks me with a domestic battery charge, sixty days in the pen, and ten months of anger management classes as if those badge motherfuckers aren't beating their ladies twice as hard on the regular."

Jack sipped his drink, slipping away into the ambient murmur of the crowded establishment. A pair of gals in upper-education merino-wool sweaters snagged the vacant stools on his other side, chattering aimlessly about their upcoming semesters and horrific Christmas dinners, spent in the company of *conservative* family membesrs who dared to publicly espouse their *conservative* opinions on abortion, an act which neither girl planned to commit, yet an act which both felt a strong compulsion to defend in honor of the abstract concept of Woman—

"So you ladies like abortions? My ex-wife and I once had an abortion. She pulled the plug, I paid the bill. The point is that I'm on your side. You ladies want drinks? Want to kick it with me and my handsome friend here?" Stevie leaned across Jack to deliver his line.

"No thanks, we're just here to talk."

"Oh come on doll, don't be uptight, the point of bars is to meet new people, right?"

Jack interjected, "Look, I'm sorry about this guy, he's three-sheets and we just met—"

"Leave us alone, fucking assholes!" She dragged her friend to a table across the room.

"Ugly ungrateful bitches." Stevie swiveled around to face his bottled jury once more. "This shithole joint has changed so much. Can't even get love from nickel broads no more. You know who Jack Ruby is? The bastard gunned down Oswald after he iced Kennedy. Commission report nonsense. Ruby's business partner used to run this place. And Lee Harvey was a certified Russophile. Think about it. This temple of post-tsarist kitsch has been crawling with feds since you were shitting your shorts, long before the scraped-knee poet-escorts and hanger-on video-store clerks moved in to stake a claim. I could spit and hit a fucking fed right now. They're everywhere, always casing the hole for raw information."

Jack turned to inspect. Stevie placed a meaty hand on his shoulder. "Don't look."

"How can you spot a fed?" Jack stammered.

Stevie's signature smirk returned. "I learned by spending the last thirty years in and around bars like this. You think that's something I can sit here and explain to a retard like you? What is this, kindergarten?" His nasty peals of laughter muzzled Jack's follow-up inquiries.

Jack swallowed his whiskey, eyes drawn again to the bold primary colors of Ukrainian pride, a stark contrast with the faded spot hidden underneath, a space remarkable only for its absence, a half-dozen of its ilk having lived and loved there before.

Unremembered rumblings from early childhood swirled drunkenly with catchy lyrical snippets, ritualized via mechanical songcraft, scoring Jack's staggered uptown jaunt to his Hell's Kitchen apartment: a foul-smelling two-bedroom sublet he pinched from a tribesman of Zion who sang showtunes part-time on cruise ships. Jack's rolodex was a verified rogues gallery of ringtop freaks, moneymen, and go-betweens, most of whom screened his calls and ignored his emails until the proper astrological configuration appeared under the canvas of Heaven.

A friendly investor, co-owner of a San Salvador hotel unreachable by land and grandson to a world-class film producer, once informed Jack that the sole long-term guarantee in the realm of job security was to make up your own unique position. Professional managers could never prick a C.E.C.C.V.C. (Creative Executive of Creatively Creating Visionary Creativity) with the pointy end of a coup, for the corporate killers wouldn't have a clue what or how much to do when the time arrived to fill the shoes.

Jack took note of his elder's advice and created a role many miles from the bushwhacked path. Clients would approach with a problem, and Jack would devise a discreet, comprehensive solution. Most satisfied buyers called him a "fixer." His current customer called Jack her "puta," a fantasy he was more than happy to oblige as long as the checks were signed and delivered on time. Amante, proponent of the ill-advised mononymous moniker, held aspirations of elevating her budding singer-songwriter career, throwing her puta a bone of a retainer each month; the young hustler tried in vain to shape reality, to spawn talent and personality from limited natural resources through an odd combination of alchemical incantations and a handful of media contacts on the up-and-coming music beat.

All the fruitless busywork in the world couldn't keep Jack from a foreboding sense of apocalypse: that the next errant doctor's visit would herald bad news, or that a near-future tropical storm might tear a hole in the sky and carry him away. Jack settled into bed with his portable sensory deprivation tools—earplugs and eye mask branded with the insignia of a mid-budget airline—and slowed his breathing, clearing negative thoughts of self-elimination.

"Change your mind, change your life," Jack affirmed under the thin iridescent glow filtering through the window shades. "I am healthy. I am whole."

The following week, a dramatic cold front came to town, bringing with it Jack's on-again, off-again mentor figure to celebrate his forty-fifth birthday in style: paying through the nose to party with a developmentally-disabled girl half his age. Ezekiel Obsidian was a washed-up scion of the independent music industry, the durable head of a well-liked boutique hip-hop label for over a decade until a ring of envious Gay Mafia underlings put him to the knives, taking advantage of a passing cultural fixation on ill-behaved antihero men who enjoyed the consenting company of younger women. Zeke grasped the essence of cool, and hopeful young starlets of the marquee at dusk flocked to his office to sing their woes in an effort to break out big. Zeke naturally treated this aspirational mass as his dating pool, and a legion of tone deaf fat chicks left in tears with twice the reason to revolt. Most importantly, Zeke taught Jack the art of the middleman; both men were adept at inserting themselves into high-value deals, making powerful introductions, and ultimately playing The Connector.

This year's shift of the screw through the month of Aquarius found Jack, Zeke, and two college co-eds sniffing their way through bags of cocaine ("Charlie") and ketamine ("Kirk") while ripping apart Zeke's hotel room in the meatpacking district.

"Doesn't it seem like all the fag clubs should be over on this side of town? A place to pack meat," Ezekiel said at the sound of speed.

"There's an old Italian film director in this area who plants his ass on a folding chair like he's working 9 to 5, smiling at ladies, a fixture of the local scene, micro-scene, calls himself the Mayor of Meatpacking. I call him the Duke of Double Entendre," Jack said.

After railing a centipede of powdered white, one of the girls, Sandra, piped in, "I talk to him every day and he's definitely not gay, always flirting with me and the other gals on our way to the hotel, he can't be less than seventy-five, incredibly virile, men only just begin to crest after forty." She crawled into Ezekiel's lap.

Jack seethed. "I agree with you in the abstract, that's why I've stopped seeking. Late twenties is a time to focus on the grind. Elevate status and the options improve. I think it's called the hypergame. The mother of my children is probably in eighth grade right now anyway."

The other girl, Susan, whined from the double bed across the room. "Which pile is coke and which is ket? This keeps fucking me up." Her voice carried a whiff of French, as though a half-decade of elite schooling on the east coast couldn't wash out the stench.

An aggressive cat, Sandra leaped at her friend, screeching, "How many times do I have to explain this, coke is a lighter off-white, just remember 'ket equals wet' because if coke were soaked it would grow darker so the ket is darker, also quit bitching, men will tolerate plenty for a nut but these guys prefer not to keep the company of literal babies."

"Fuck you, bitch! This idiot just said he wanted to impregnate a middle-schooler!"

Jack glanced at Zeke, his mien seeming to ask *why do we do this to ourselves?* The older man offered a crude sexual hand gesture in return, fingers curling for the dripping currency worth more to him than liquid gold.

Jack rolled his eyes, for once totally turned off. "Hey Susan, where are you from?"

"The United States of America," she deadpanned.

"Oh that's just wonderful, I'm slated to spend next month in Berlin and I'm looking for lodging recommendations from a bonafide European, sorry to pester a true blue daughter of the revolution like you."

Susan indulged him. "My cousin is coming to New York for a spell, his flat will be empty for all four weeks of February, I'll connect you two."

Jack whipped out a small notebook and a ballpoint pen. "Splendid, what's your email?"

Jack passed the days with little deviation from a routine of his own making, the lone light of sanity in the face of frigid January weather: steeped tea and diaristic contemplation in the AM, professional communications and business development in the PM, with a sober sojourn into town somewhere after dark to meet a "friend," the definition of the word reduced to "contact," "lead," "fence" or "mark." Recent nights of rampant debauchery had left Jack feeling hollow and alone by morning, so he decided to set aside the sauce in favor of a more authentic experience: namely, taking a weekend stroll down one hundred and eleven Manhattan city blocks, tripping not on the uneven concrete but instead on a manageable dose of psilocybin mushrooms, colliding not with poorly-placed traffic cones but instead with an irritating young theater producer and his understudy girlfriend, who was very popular with the other lads when she danced. Jack avoided exposing his altered mind and proceeded south on 5th Avenue.

Sick of see-sawing between monotony and oblivion, a hole in the social matrix where a man once stood, Jack's luck changed that very Friday, the 13th, during a long day's journey into night that began with hot coffee in a hotel lobby on the east side. Ezekiel, kicked out of his previous digs due to perpetual noise complaints and profound structural damage, ditched Sandra—or maybe it unfolded like Opposite Day—and took up residence in a more dignified historic traveler's haunt for one final night before returning to Hollywood.

"I can't believe I could have been in Russia right now. Fuck the war-averse sensibilities of the majors," Jack said, reiterating a worn-out story about how he *almost* secured a six-month gig managing Na$tio, the breakout sensation of a fertile Slavic disco culture thanks to a minor temporal rift, quietly brushed under the Bessarabian rug by CERN, which created lagging pop music trends when traveling east through the timezones: Thailand only recently discovered Thelonious Monk.

"Fuck that total hack Na$tio too. I co-produced a couple of early singles. He's a fame-hungry brat who coasts on the talent of his session players," Ezekiel said.

The hotel's barista approached their table with angry footfalls and two to-go cups which barely obscured her dour expression.

"You're supposed to wait for your order, these have been chilling on the counter for almost twenty minutes."

"We're so sorry about that—"

"He doesn't speak for me." Ezekiel spun his finger in a circle to indicate the other patrons. "This lot seems to be worthy of table service, in your finest mugs too. And I don't intend on drinking chilled coffee on a chilly day. Mind trying again?"

Shocked at his candor in a crowd of dead-eyed floaters, the barista apologized for singling them out and hurried back to remake their cappuccinos. A renowned actor of stage and screen—on trial uptown for manslaughter after a mishap with a samurai sword and a martini shot that was supposed to break the fourth wall rather than decapitate the cameraman—walked past their table, unshaven, haggard, bodyguard in tow.

"Was that . . . ?"

"Yeah."

"I need a cigarette."

Ezekiel and Jack landed on their feet outside, puffing on lit darts, the elder man querying his protégé. "How's your docket this year?"

"Amante has that grand masquerade at the end of the month, I'm helping out with a bit of organizing. Next month is the big new music convention in Germany, a feeder for Eurovision if cards are played right. I'd really like to sow some seeds and manufacture an It Girl, one with a superior value system than all these pornstars and camgirls and ran-through podcasters."

Ezekiel ashed his cigarette and nodded. "I might join you in Berlin, likely a wise opportunity to fundraise." He was deep in development on a startup with a proprietary method of dissemination for independent musicians, a hit factory to shatter the spines of the dinosaurs. Jack caught a check for some light consulting, explaining in bitter terms the incestuous relationship between legacy reporters and label reps, a pair of guards to gatekeep the microphone.

Jack watched a black hatchback swerve to avoid flattening an errant cyclist, consumed by the jihadist impulse to cut across two traffic lanes and join his tarp salesman brethren in praying towards the alleged holy land. The ginger lady behind the wheel nearly transformed the patio seating of a mid-range Mexican restaurant into a freshly-dug mass grave. Pressure from city officials to replace each available parallel parking space with the plastic ephemera of "outdoor dining"—slamming red-sauce pozoles while squatting on a slab of street concrete under the watchful eye of garçon-gestapo guaranteed *at least* a twenty-percent gratuity—had increased non-choking dinner deaths and afternoon congestion by non-negligible margins.

"Want to grab a bite?"

"Not at this time, thank you."

Ezekiel rolled with the rejection, opting to retire to his room for a siesta 'til dusk. With a wish to avoid overpriced carnitas and roadside carnage, Jack fled to his pad to cook chicken, onions and rice. That's a meat, a vegetable and a starch, for those nutritionists criticizing from the couch. His belly full, Jack dodged needy beggars and greedy vagrants on his path back to that little slice of cinema heaven on Ludlow, strolling in five minutes late to some '70s picture about the civil servants of the New York City underground transit system and their companions in emergency services, the whole bureaucratic gang trying to foil a coldly-executed hijacking, as if to imply that holding hands and singing "We Are The World" would reverse the decline of the West. Jack caught the giggles in the third row, the mainstay IF I'D BEEN THERE IT WOULD HAVE GONE DOWN DIFFERENTLY meme looping in his skull, the pot edible he forgot he had swallowed beginning to express its hysterical effects. The movie concluded with a Q&A session between two running mouths whose names failed to emerge in the crawl of credits, dunking the onscreen events in a contemporary gloss to discuss racial tension and the lack of women in the workforce.

A stock ringtone and a vibrating pant-leg dragged Jack away from the glares of the audience, their hands in starting positions to launch asinine inquiries about the state of Metropolitika in America. He slipped into the taxi waiting curbside.

Ezekiel clapped his ward on the shoulder. "We're headed far uptown, I found this crew of backpack rappers who squat in the unfinished basement of an American Legion on the whisper's edge of Harlem. Could be strong leads for new clients."

The car snaked along the highway bordering the East River, a room with a view on wheels. Jack spotted a towering neon sign that simply read GOOD. In a beat, it disappeared, an interborough mirage.

"How did you sniff out these guys? Is the music any good?" Jack politely declined a coke spoon beneath the eyeline of the driver's mirror.

Ezekiel snorted a fat bump. "They have yet to publish a single demo, the guys share admin duties on a social page, reposting test scores with snarky commentary appended to the top. They follow someone who follows me and the intermediary forwarded some material then set me up with an address and a time to meet. It's a party, should be casual."

After arriving at the spot, Jack followed Ezekiel past a grimy doorframe that descended into a cavernous room likely zoned as non-residential space. An assortment of adolescent whites sporting hip-hop hoodies and basketball shorts idled around a folding card table crowned with two department-store handles of clear rum. Three gals, all girlfriends, faded into the crowd like low-end optical illusions. Jack thought he recognized a stop on his former route home, a chick who used to fill him with lab-grade speed before gagging herself with his equipment; then he remembered that she had moved to Gulf Shores to suck professionally on yachts.

The crew's ringleader, nineteen-year-old Dot, jumped up to greet the newcomers.

"Yoooo, is that Mr. Obsidian? The doctor is *here* taking *patients!*"

Dot wrapped Ezekiel in a clumsy bear hug, smothering the older man's glance towards Jack that seemed to suggest instant regret in joining these down 'n' out hoodrat festivities, a portal opened from the suburban South. Dot released Ezekiel and sized up Jack.

"This is my friend and ally, Jack Valentine, the invisible man greasing his puppet-master strings." Ezekiel could adopt the local parlance, a country-boy stew of empty idiom and utter gibberish, with ease.

Dot manipulated Jack's right hand with two full seconds of esoteric dap, a bump and a slap and a pound and a clap. "Come in fellas, come in, get comfy, grab a chair if four-legs is the measure of your pride and joy."

A lard bucket with jerry curls occupied the only seat in sight, practicing a preacher's sermon repeating "by the blood of Christ" into his vocoder as though he were Mr. Delta Blues himself.

Dot addressed the room. "This ancient dog ran Maelstrom Records for like a century, the brightest and highest guided by his hand on to—"

"Let's take shotsssss," Dot's girlfriend cut him off.

"Shut up bitch I'm tryna talk!"

"That's a killer drop, run it back and I'll bust out the sampler," some crony chimed in from the teeming throngs of underage drunks.

Ezekiel picked up the discarded thread, ever eager to toot his own horn. "Maelstrom was the top of the buffet, salad days, but I'm in the sweet tooth era now, what are you boys baking?"

Another crony arranged two dozen disposable cups and poured double jiggers of liquor in each, a supersized Last Sipper for the dawn of a new age.

"The memes are flowing fast, it's nearly a full-time job even split six ways. We're focused on intake, listening to all the goods from real musicians like real musicians should. If it's been reviewed on *Treble Every Day*, guaran-fuckin'-teed we've absorbed its highs, lows, and mids. Our taste is our coin. A proper release will come, maybe next year. Inshallah."

Third- and fourth-string cronies distributed the cherry solos, sloshing with corner-store poison. Jack politely declined, earning the ire of the drink attendant, who yelled, "Yo come on pussy, have a little sip with your boys here."

Ezekiel sank into a cozy corner with the only available chick after she held up her phone with winking admiration to demonstrate that they were already connected online.

Jack sighed. "Hey buddy, I gotta ride out and use this ticket for a midnight DJ set in Williamsburg."

Ezekiel scrambled to his feet and told Dot he'd be in touch before joining Jack in the crisp winds of the upper-upper west. Two more cigarettes graced the duo's lips. Ezekiel offered his sidewalk review of the oil-slick kickback.

"That was certainly an earnest pack of retards."

The fragmentary delivery of information across the internet's superhighway trickled down from interstate infrastructure to dirt backroads where niche communities dwell, lining the edge of the woods, waiting with crowbars to knock off an eighteen-wheeler that stopped to clear a log, repurposing the consumer electronics inside for ends either noble or nefarious, a subculture on the fringe of a subculture. Youth coming of age in the century of acceleration mastered the means of dissemination years before failing high-school economics, their organized memetic spread weaponized to tear down soothsayers and ayatollahs alike, a cause championed by slouching activists who see only uppercuts instead of directionless chaos, a competition to garner the greatest laugh from the least developed frontal lobe. These kids were weaned on hip-hop beef and war crime walkthroughs and will inherit the earth.

"You seemed to be enjoying yourself near the end, students can slobber over their creative brilliance as long as a little drool lands on teacher, right?"

High as a kite off powdered white, Ezekiel fired back. "They're savvy and apolitical, that fusion of traits has its benefits, plus that girl gave me her direct line, what's eating you?"

Participation trophies, a long-term soft shibboleth of ideological feuds, ascended to newfound authority overlooking the arts: You Made Something, Therefore It Must Be Good.

"Time and attention are finite resources. Where's the talent? Are these really our people?" Jack swallowed his harshest critique, choice words about the social evaporation of that autist Sandra and Zeke's natural displacement into a comparable collection of irritating teens.

"The rolodex knows no bounds, and there is a hierarchy, with recent company notched near the bottom. You said there's some event to scoot to? Let's go?"

Jack rubbed the sour from his eyes and stifled a mild yawn. "The gig is sold out, and these early-morning rises are catching up to me. I can slide you my ticket if you want to head south and scout." He unfolded the paperslip printout from his jacket pocket, the Times New Roman ad-copy promoting the recent release of a literary magazine known for religious cosplay and banal musical acts needle-dropping hyperpop oldies.

Ezekiel groaned. "Not my speed."

Jack's dilemma revolved less around the lateness of the hour—he carried emergency adderall in a secret coat pocket for just this reason—and more the immense journey from 132nd St. across the bridge to Brooklyn, passing his home stop along the way, all in the name of what? Awkward two-stepping to bad tunes and a handful of phone numbers he'd never use after the obligatory exchange of first and last names? Pessimism killed his ancestors, and Jack's sense of veneration for the deeply dead was surprisingly strong, so he bid adieu to Ezekiel for this trip and descended the length of Manhattan on the C.

Like a half-remembered act of sheer intemperance, a young antihero performing on a different stage glided through the metro after picking two locks and before making quick work of two more, a shimmering teenage transvestite, black of skin and blue of dress. Jack's eyes glazed over, caught staring at advertisements, warnings about lead-coated baby bottles alongside promos encouraging home-delivery abortion, both adorned in the color palette of hypermillennial restauranteering.

His ex—the last, nearly fatal, who described his first gift to her, a silken wardrobe item turned piece of movie memorabilia, as "a blouse for the Devil's whore"—once brought him a computer printout of a template contract to ensure he'd cover his cut of the terminated pregnancy; no conversation or debate, only paperwork and shoddy legalese. Her finger lay on the trigger of her smartphone, ready to blow up his social life should he decline to palm her two hundred bucks of blood money. She was a Faustian harlot named Charlotte, and their relationship burned to a crisp in a series of grocery store parking lots after an explosive incident that began with an argument over blowjobs and cinematography and ended with a shoe hurled through the rear window of a shiny new sedan. It was actually their second abortion, though Jack's state-of-mind on moral matters had shifted right in between that safe-legal-rare pair. For a culture too timid to riff on death, the West seemed to worship the void, sacrificing the youngest and the oldest to its gaping maw and receiving high-speed 4K streaming and on-demand global cuisine in return.

Jack transferred to the J and earned an eyeline of lit skyline, praise be to the above-ground tram. Marcy, the first stop in a fresh borough, sat above the standard smoke shops and bodegas, check-cashing institutions and franchise eateries, bathing their burgers in the glow of LED menu screens. This side of the East River felt immediately less glamorous, the electricity of streets on a grid system swapped for dark patches of elevated danger without a boost in thrills. Jack strolled towards the venue, the same one selected for every scene party hoping for a whiff of legitimacy, save for those with untouchable names on the bill. He spotted a self-infantilizing Asian girl—in frilly white lace following handheld GPS like she was geocaching in the midst of near-future water wars—and knew he was headed in the correct direction. A gaggle of hipsters and a handful of teeny-boppers stood around the entrance, rival gangs ripping stogies and sweet-flavored vapes, respectively. Jack presented his ticket to the meathead manning the door. A mildly popular nymph of a playwright with a prominent nose floated past, recognizing him.

"Let's see some ID."

"We still need to get that coffee."

Two requests, imperative in their own fashion, arrived simultaneously in each of Jack's ears, surround sound for the everyday commuter. In lieu of a little-used driver's license, he flashed a twenty-dollar note, access granted by the post-gold currency snatched and walleted by the rent-a-guard. Once inside, Jack made the rounds on brisk feet, passing a trifecta of bars slinging price-jacked cocktails to crowds of stupefied drinking pals. Pitched-up vocals over a frenetic machine beat echoed from the front room's dance floor.

"I don't give a fuck if you're trans, TURN DOWN THE BPM!"

Jack wandered towards the source of the music, hanging his coat on a spare hook to enter the fray with the lightness to move, to shake, to spin, and to gawk at pretty girls until they read the room and started gently rubbing their doll parts on his jeans. He danced with one gal, an ambassador from the goth subculture with hair like death and chest like torpedoes. Their idle chatter filled dead air in the mix until she abruptly evacuated the premises. Out of sight, out of mind, out of bladder space: Jack quested through the bodily sea for the bathroom, derailed along the way by one of the hosts, a blonde with a prominent nose who once gushed to see him when it felt advantageous to her juvenile magazine, offering only frigid greetings after his utility ran dry.

"Cool party," Jack lied.

"Uh . . . thanks."

"You going to Amante's big masquerade later this month?"

"Uh . . . no thanks, I totally dig the Magna Carta, plus those people are fascist elitists."

By the fury of his mind, Jack pressed onwards to the toilets, passing a lanky finance type with a neanderthalic gal on his arm, both digging greedily into a dimebag of blow.

A braindead initiator echoed through Jack's skull. "Don't worry, I'm not a fed."

The tall guy didn't break eye contact with the powder. "Exactly what a fed would say."

Inside the stall, Jack cycled through a dialogue tree of asinine retorts, from something about entrapment to Don't Worry, I Won't Tell Your Mom Either: *l'esprit de l'urinoir*. He reengaged with a true-blue canned favorite once the men's room door swung open.

"Can I trouble you for a bump?"

Contrary to traditional gift-giving, the chief problem with drugs mooched and bummed was one of gratitude, a freebie for the price of conversation with a tormentor who chewed your ear clean off for the next twenty minutes in a dusty basement corner by the staff locker room. These two— Adam and Gwen (not Eve [or Steve])—proved to be rather normal, querying Jack on his professional pursuits. He spun a story about a legendary indie-folk songsman, sandblasted from the internet for popularizing skeptical, "conspiratorial" thinking on the topic of those grating seatbelt alarm beeps hardwired into newer cars, a minor method of subliminal control obvious to anyone who didn't vacuum bugs with their mouth for biweekly pay; Jack helped mount a campaign for his comeback EP.

Gwen was a fan. "Haven't listened to recent stuff, but I read that article in *The Gazette.*"

Jack smiled. "Always nice to meet an enthusiast. I placed that piece. Don't repeat this, but the paper's editor is the retarded cousin of the publisher's son." He could horsetrade like it was still that glorious year before the Model T.

"Fucking nepobabies." Adam hit the bag again. "Clean out the cribs!"

"Get real, you'd be licking the toes of the first trust-fund bitch who struts in barefoot," Gwen said.

The three of them leaned tight against the cracked wallpaper. Various pissers and snorters flowed in and out of the stalls, a middle passage of waste and depravity. Jack led Gwen and Adam to a spot across from the merch table, garish snapbacks and downloadable MP3s on business cardstock piled at elbow height. Adam slurped his can of beer. Gwen puffed on her vape, managing to appear small-town doe-eyed towards the surrounding social frame and utterly bored with the portrait within. A rough blonde sized up Jack, who did the dignified deed and gave a toothy grin right back.

"You have magnificent teeth, is that from regular treatments?"

Jack's dentist had lambasted his efforts for nearly two decades, the scolding stare of a masked schoolmarm blotting out the harsh examination light, central orifice pinned open by plastic spreaders and tortuous metal tools while the chilling noise of daytime television invaded his ears, the "witty" banter and royalty-free tunage of home renovation meets marriage counseling programs sponsored by cardboard modernist developers—until he learned to properly floss.

"I bought a stash of boxed whitening strips and went to town."

"I'm shook, you straight up look like a '90s Brad Pitt."

An old comparison, a kind compliment; Jack thanked her nonetheless.

Under the spell of liquid hops, Adam chimed in. "He's single!"

Jack cringed. "I didn't put him up to that, we just met—"

"I'm not!" Her closing remark, a lingering mushroom cloud.

Without missing a beat, another blonde glided in to fill the space, a performative backwoods lilt coating her opener. "Well *I'm* single!"

She shimmied her shoulders to-and-fro with almost ironic erotic flair, an Olde Hollywood starlet playing herself in a romantic farce. Her clothes were baggy, someone transitioning from a plaid suitcase to a crawlspace apartment. Jack hardly noticed, as her cheerful disposition congregated around a magnificent centerpiece: the most beautiful smile he'd ever seen, outpacing catalogs and camera tests and billboards and broadsheets, tucked inside a soft face fit for the pictures. She laughed with her whole body at some private amusement, a magic giggle releasing shockwaves of pure light. Her psychic power was immense, stretching past the ceiling of any traditional chart; in a room, a city, a planet teeming with vacant shells on autopilot, this was a *real* woman, someone choosing to play the game with the same limitless rules as him.

Gwen blew a fat cloud of nicotine and made the introduction. "This is Penny. She moved to New York last week."

Adam continued his obnoxious tirade. "Fresh meat! You wanna get with her?"

"I'm Jack Valentine. Where'd you come from, cowgirl?"

"Ohio, my angel, where the tomatoes grow plump on the vine."

Tickled pink, Penny's generosity of mirth made Jack feel mighty special, one lucky customer, the king of comedy, even if this turned out to be her default mode of interaction.

"We're all from that neck of the Midwest," Gwen added.

"I'm a Georgia boy at heart. If we join forces, we can transform this archipelago of WASPs into a white trash wonderland."

The venue's house lights sparked to life. Overhead illumination at this time of night had a sobering effect on swaying trees and bootyshakers, a 60-watt palace guard protecting pairs and squares from the folly of regrettable sexscapades by lobbing one last question in their path to the exit: "now that you can see past the ass through the eyes to the soul, do you *really* want to sloppily fuck this stranger?"

Splendid and uncharacteristic good fortune brought Jack instead to this gang of respectable boys and girls whose lone collective desire while spilling out into the street was to pillage a corner store for shooters and tallboys to keep the party alive. Loud, persistent chatter on the best direction for their trek attracted both the ire of building security and a handful of new followers to the caravan, including a skinwalker with shoulder-length locks who seemed immediately enamored with Jack.

"Someone texted me the details to the afters if you want to split off and check it out."

Jack quickly and deliberately echoed the plan to Penny (primarily), Adam and Gwen (to a lesser extent), and a couple of stragglers (price paid for non-specific vocalization), the whole group marching further east in lockstep. Gwen and Penny clucked like mother hens, finding joy on repeat through a promotional billfold that could be unrolled like a scroll and matched with imagined Roman decrees, a dependable laugh earned from Jack nearly every time. The ladies were dressed optimistically, rags and feathers for warmer weather. Each keybump brought fresh hostility from Adam, instructing them to shut their traps and calling them retards. They sang protest songs and prayed for his health.

The longhair in the Columbine coat sauntered up two sets of steps, trying the apparent door code, then buzzing A4 to no avail. Another hanger-on took over as conductor, leading the gathered lot towards oblivion, Other People's Booze by the bucketload based on stale intel, a bunk address, an exaggerated invitation. If ten paces made a duel, perhaps ten-hundred could make a party. Jack's beeline towards Penny's side was blocked by the creature from the boy/girl lagoon.

"Do you like living in New York?"

Jack's southern hospitality failed to launch with a factory reset. "I sure do."

"Do you like movies?"

"Yep."

After hours, the best returned home, and the rest lurked near stoops and empty alleyways, nursing shared sixteen-ounce bottles of beer, disease and drug free. Gwen and Penny glanced over their respective shoulders at Jack, who smirked and shouted, "I don't remember the trail of tears being this tough."

More giggles from the girls. Hard to parse whether their frothy exhales were produced by low-end temperatures or vaporized nicotine, a fourth-grade science-fair project changing liquid to gas in three inches or less. The sky opened, and ashy flakes of snow descended from on high. Penny twirled and moaned.

"Pompeii is *burning*."

She seemed to bear the gift of divine knowledge, an angelic messenger outside of time and memory, thy kingdom cometh with a warning of stormlands a-brewing. Could she, too, feel the tingle of static on the tips of her fingers? Was the cursèd realm beneath Mount Vesuvius a similar land of decadence, degeneracy and decline? Before the inferno, what sorts of psyops and false flags planned on dry parchment had contributed to the fall?

The group loitered outside a ground-floor apartment: another set of tenants inclined to greet the all-night crew with abject silence, the only sound this close to Hasidic Brooklyn a tight grouping of unanswered knocks. The assembly began to splinter. Jack tightened his parka, cold-blooded and too tall for pumped red cells to reach his extremities.

"I suppose that's my cue."

Gwen and a couple of the weird follow-on guys held out their smartphones expectantly, begging for his Instagram handle. He told the truth, delivering his spiel about techno-liberation and brainrot and paranoid playmates. The people said what the people always say, a mix of admiration and jealousy, yet reluctance to take the leap and delete their digital personalities. Jack eyed Penny and weighed the calculus of singling her out for a phone number exchange, risking contact info runoff in the unfortunate direction of the present creeps. Penny asked if he was going to Heaven tomorrow. He assumed that to be another party joint and said no, but he looked forward to another road to nowhere with her in the future.

Jack lounged in the folds of his comforter and eavesdropped on his roommate, who was running lines for an upcoming audition. The guy next door stressed each godforsaken syllable to the point of fracture, telegraphing the emotional subtext of the script through the stratosphere into a coliseum of extraterrestrial viewers surrounding the earth's stage. Bad actors earned jobs by the mettle of their network, managing to appear on screens nationwide in front of butts flocking to box-office-tallied seats, but to lack talent *and* wallow in obscurity was a fate worse than fleeting fame. In his youth, Jack spent time in a secondary market bullpen of background performers, people who pantomimed like hooked fish in the deep bokeh of crowded wide shots then breathlessly cited their "incredible experience collaborating with Dwaynetherockjohnson on his latest project." Aspiration run awry made easy targets for glass-shattering dunks, and Jack's chief co-conspirator in those days was his old pal Rose, an actress of a higher caliber currently suspended a mile above the eastern seaboard on her way to visit him in New York.

Rose was a funny dyke, a chapstick lesbian, her sported swag reminding him of preteen boys in baseball caps who liked to skateboard and maybe circlejerk, but not in a gay way. Her levity won her the instant admiration of many a curious straight girl, sorority outcasts and men's club service staff who appreciated the opportunity to have their rugs munched without the obligatory "my turn" grin of supine dudes. Desire to play dress-up with a lady lover lasted about as long as a young filly's dollhouse phase, leaving Rose down bad for a revolving door of dumb blondes and fickle broads.

Outside of her inability to select suitable romantic matches, Rose benefitted from outstanding interpersonal intelligence. For a year and some change, Jack and Rose recorded an inflammatory rush hour radio show under pseudonyms, discussing current events and larger political trends with biting satirical bent and bad-faith interpretations, offending all sides in equal measure. Their special sauce was riling up first-time callers with a moronic soundboard, aiming to anger Joe Q. Public in ninety seconds flat or the listener's money back.

After a brief reminiscence about their hijinks, Jack escorted Rose to a revered two-story haunt on west 52nd, a dark red Russian dinner joint with borscht-infused vodka and a grand piano taking song requests for cents on the dollar. Jack had ventured here two weeks ago with a junior associate who managed investments for a family office that was eager to dump cash into underground music with a pro-marriage message. Last week he dined alone, scribbling inward-facing observations while former mail-order beauty queens waited hand 'n' foot on small-time mobsters and twenty-top Broadway strike celebrations. That night, a weekend, he and Rose barely squeezed into a doorside table. Hollow stares of Eastern Eurotrash, conspiring in their first languages, greeted them from the impenetrable abyss within.

Rose was content and stimulated, sipping a cucumber martini reflecting the wall-mount TV set playing bonehead action flicks from the early aughts. The faux Tiffany lampshade created an aesthetic delight when juxtaposed with the tube, a kitschy tableau meant to accent the environment, not drain the focus away from the three-piece swing ensemble. Rose snapped a still-life video with her camera phone, activating Jack's early-warning anti-tech alarm system.

"Please don't do that in a place like this."

Rose whipped around, knocking a couple drops of Jack's decaf onto the grateful saucer. "What are you talking about? Don't tell me what to do."

"I'm serious, we're attracting attention, best to blend in."

"I don't care what these random fucking people think, I'm enjoying myself and will want to remember this fondly when I look at my photo archive later. Stop trying to control me."

Off stern glances from strangers, Jack pivoted to hushed tones. "You're making a scene. I hang out here on the regular and don't want to be seen as a stupid gawking tourist."

The hostess appeared from the hidden backrooms. "Where you two lovebirds from?"

Jack glared at Rose and leaped on the grenade. "I live here, she's visiting from Georgia. We're not together—"

A glint of recognition. "My cousin move to Tbilisi during war. What is names?"

Rose pointed towards herself—"Rose"—then her booth partner: "Jack."

The hostess smiled. "Is nice, very nice, like sinking boat movie. Sad!"

Museum Mile, off the eastern edge of Central Park, was inappropriately named, as the true tally of steps required to navigate those half-dozen mausoleums—the winding corridors, the unmapped wings, the capsule descriptions penned by graduate students eager to recontextualize art narratives based on wishy-washy notions of social justice— numbered closer to a half-marathon, far too many for a single afternoon outing. Rose, seeking to maximize her island time despite learnèd, sensible protest from her host, dragged Jack through a bevy of both temporary exhibits and permanent collections as though he were a leashed child at a turn-of-the-century CPAC.

His consolation prize came in a sub-basement of the Metropolitan. Jack was struck dumb by a set of paintings depicting the sixteenth century Beeldenstorm of Northern Europe, wherein impoverished Protestant rebels sacked the glorious Catholic churches of their betters in an iconoclastic campaign against beauty, a Platonic ideal charred at the stake to make way for the stark stucco walls of younger, community-theater denominations. He inked a dotted line between the artistic destruction at the end of the Dark Ages and his own generation's obsession with deleting browser history, then cringed at his pseudo-profound observation, then pondered why the gallery placards for once failed to mention any contemporary comparisons, neither statues torn asunder nor even an easy, apolitical reference to books banned or burned.

Rose spooked him from around the corner. "I've run out of drive space for fine art, my retinas won't transmit any more data. Find anything of note down here?"

Jack spread his hands to indicate the present section, palms up, a maître d' proud to be part of the three-star team. "Aesthetic enrichment and a lesson from olde, what's not to like?"

To repay Rose for her daylight jaunt across the spent endowments of cultural non-profit institutions, Jack whisked his weekend ward downtown to the Soviet bar. A gentle introduction to the usual crowd of indie movie producers and associated below-the-line beatniks might benefit her budding career on the small screen. Thanks to the gutting of the theatrical window by studio executives—greedy, adaptable, who could say—all media had shrunk accordingly.

Rose reclined in her high-rise stool, a balancing act for any citizen over five feet tall. Jack ordered them whiskeys-on-ice, having decided recently that a drunken romp one night per week surely carried a variety of physical, social, and emotional rewards. Rose chatted casually with a world-class cinematographer and soon had his whole posse beating their knees into paste, cackling at her self-deprecating style. Jack kept his head on a swivel, searching for the idle comfort of conversation with someone, anyone he already knew, finding a two-headed blessing, faintly recognized, seated among fast friends in a booth: Gwen and Adam, from the other night.

Jack sauntered over. Gwen scrunched her brows. "Oh! It's you. We were all trying to remember your name the next day. We asked around Heaven, no luck. You're a mystery man!"

Jack savored the delayed attention. "Jack. Rhymes with crack, but I'm no addict."

Adam quickly hogged the speaking stick, relaying with river-rapid syncopation a ten-minute shaggy dog story based on a rumor from a scenester blog.

"And the worst part is, the feng shui was entirely pseudonymous!"

Jack nodded politely, his eye contact unwavering. Rose shouted for him to meet her in the bathroom, and he joined her in the stall with two big-boned geeks whom she had been leading on for free blow, slyly fueling their desire for an Eiffel Tower that could crush her into cornmeal.

Coked out and thirsty, Jack rang up another round of whiskeys and returned to Gwen. "What's up with your homegirl that just blew into town?"

Gwen glanced at Adam. They shared a knowing laugh. "She's a musician amassing colorful lore fast. Look up Penny Delphine and poke around when you get home."

Jack scrawled the presumed stage name in his notebook, eager to learn the lay of her heartlands, and punched his digits into Gwen's cell, citing group dinner plans manufactured on the spot for later in the week. He spied his old friend nearing an altercation across the room—some pretentious film editor preferred to limit access to the hot girls in his immediate orbit, pissing in the drink of down-to-earth Rose, who raised her tiny fist intending to do damage—and tugged the little firebrand out the door into a taxi to ferry them home. The driver claimed to love his job, more a daisy chain of one-off contract gigs for backseat bosses. Fond of fibbing while tipsy, Rose informed the driver that Jack loved his job too, as a professional clown.

"You mean like a comedian or something?"

"Sure, physical comedy, like the brothers Marx but elevated."

Jack picked up the thread. "I had a car accident last year, the doctor said I broke my funny bone and couldn't work."

The driver missed their next turn. "Did you need surgery?"

Rose repacked her utilitarian camise: socks and briefs, tanks and sweats for a short trip. Jack clocked in for a shift of internet sleuthing, the name Penny Delphine filling his search bar. He found a collection of demo tracks and clicked play, unleashing the sound of rough acoustic tinkering anchored by the haunted multi-octave wail of a gal who'd seen some trouble. The male brain, unable to process lyrics without an explanation or a sheet of liner notes, nevertheless picked out choice selections that seemed to scratch at thematic intent, odes to incels and lamentations of rape with sprinkled references to theology and classical myth.

"What the fuck is that screeching?" Rose chimed in from the bedroom.

Jack ignored her untrained ear, savoring Penny's raw talent, an unteachable quality easily supplemented by increased production value and the mystic art of marketing. Her songs, even as bare sketches, spoke with awe of end days upon us, the eschatology of biblical revelation rendered through witty turns-of-phrase and poetic profundity. This was pure spirit, powerful and kindred. Jack was smitten, personally and professionally.

Her cabin bag shouldered, Rose joined him in the living room. Jack stood tall to perform the goodbye ritual, hugs and promises to return midway through the year.

"Did you hear my question? That sounded terrifying."

Jack smiled. "I feel like I found a hundred dollar bill lying on the ground."

Rose smiled back, an act of mimicry, not of knowing. She departed for the Jersey-side airport. Jack tabbed back to his browser's search results and discovered a message board thread with hundreds of likes and comments titled "There's some retard running around Ohio calling herself Penny Delphine..." The post went on to describe how Penny D., presumably the one and only, was fond of opening her open-mic sets with proclamations mourning the legion of aborted babies lining the country's wastebins, "those tragic unborn children numbering greater than the Jews murdered in the Holocaust," an act which led to a blanket ban from regional dive bars, her "midwit Appalachian cabaret act" chased out of town by the sharp end of liberal pitchforks.

Jack wasn't exactly exiled from his birthplace down south, though a cabal of ex-girlfriends hexed him for misbehaving before he could evacuate that incestuous music scene. He had moved to New York on a whim after visiting, claiming to wish to explore "greater creative opportunities," yet actually hounding after Amelia, a twenty-year-old rich girl whose parents had her cloistered in Tribeca after she got addicted to smack during a Shakespeare conservatory in London. He met her on a thin-excuse for a hookup app, their first date spent shotgunning beers in a winter park then dancing to hard transexual techno in the catacombs beneath an out-of-service factory, photography discouraged by black stickers slapped on phone cameras. When their fiendish hunt for blow went belly-up, Amelia flashed nearly five hundred dollars in cash that she "found" in her jacket pocket, forking it over to Jack to book a trashy chain hotel room for them to stain with lust. Their second date included more drunken two-stepping and a mixed collection of anonymous cokeheads railing lines in a different burnt motel room, concluding with a territorial debate gone bust and a glass bong smashed across the faces of the perceived intruders, bleeding on carpet that had probably absorbed worse 'til an ambulance arrived. Jack decluttered his material life and shipped up to NYC a half-month later, never quite managing to lock down that wild child for a third date.

His long Grim Reaper fingers stretched into action, screenshotting the callout post for posterity, then flagging it for moderator removal, citing "personal information that compromises my identity" and signing the message as Penny, ticking the box for "hate speech" to add weight to his forum complaint. Breaking into the mainstream pop landscape would require a delicate balance between values and respectability to avoid an immediate public relations crisis.

Jack flipped open his cell and methodically composed a t9 text to Gwen, inviting her and "the recent transplant" to a Thursday-evening dinner at a popular French eatery on the corner of 1st Ave and Houston. She responded within seconds—whether due to excitement or as a byproduct of already staring into the abyss of her phone, he couldn't be sure—with a positive RSVP for two.

Not one to suffer overactive nerves on the eve of a planned encounter with a beautiful woman, even when a pair of queens slid his way from the deck, Jack nevertheless popped a pot gummy. The clear view through a sativa plant enabled greater latitude of wit and the slow, assured cadence of a diplomat.

"When politicians toke a common blunt, it's known as the world peace pipe." His practiced post-delivery facial expression needed a light upgrade. An off-kilter mouth corner appeared in the speckled mirror, suggesting a hunter's smile, not a jester's grin. The material was a grade below dollar-store joke-book bathroom-reader, but he could fumble his way through a group hang, no square-dance scandal here.

Jack wandered south on the A, then put boots to concrete the rest of the way east, allowing time for the edible to ignite. He walked past a hysterical woman of millennial age, too clean and pampered to be a bum, yet screaming with operatic lung strength all the same: "COME BACK! COME BACK OR I'LL FUCKING KILL MYSELF!"

Shaken by the desperation but not stirred to intervene, Jack merely gawked from across the street. The perpetual motion machine of his feet refused to stop for any old rusted coin on the pavement. He arrived outside the bistro a cool ten minutes late, spotting Gwen and the mythical songbird by her side, waiting to be seated in the packed establishment.

"Is that Penny Delphine in the effervescent flesh?"

She blushed on command, turning to Gwen with screentest surprise. "Were you two talking about little old me?"

Her friend shrugged, indifferent. Penny wore black tights under a shapely purple dress with an elegant white collar.

"I like your style, on the mic and off."

Penny's eyes opened wide, from asiatic to anime. "I need to delist those demos!"

"I suppose I'm the lucky last guy to hear 'em." Jack extended his neck to glance inside the restaurant. "What's the hold-up? There's always a spare table in the back. Hold tight."

He snatched Penny's hand, she grabbed Gwen's, and he pulled them both past the crowded doorway. The bar was gilded, the floor was checkered, and the thin path between glorious front and cramped rear remained blocked by an irritated waitress.

Jack laid on the charm. "Can we squeeze in somewhere?"

Another waitress clanged coins into the tray, counting zinc and copper with grandmother's patience. The gatekeeper sighed—"I guess"—and escorted the trio to a booth tucked out of sight.

Jack stripped off his oversized parka. "Do you have coat check?"

The waitress hesitated. "No…" She clocked Jack's persuasive smile. "…But I can stash these in the basement, if you'd like."

She expected them to decline; Jack nodded, pleased to be rid of his winter burden for an hour or two. Gwen and Penny sat opposite each other. Jack slid into the booth next to Penny, their legs forced to touch ever so gently beneath the table. He ordered wine and mussels, for three, and accented the accidental choice of aphrodisiacs with bad dad wordplay: something something don't "whine" if you've got "muscles" to spare, etc. The ladies laughed despite this side of low-hanging fruit.

Gwen described the nuances distinguishing *manifestation* from *manic infestation*. Penny punctuated her friend's monologue with violent pantomime, pretending to machine gun the surrounding food hall and making the appropriate Uzi sounds with her luscious lips.

"Sometimes a schizoid rampage feels like the only way to fight the decade's decay."

"We could gun 'em down together. Jack and Penny rolls off the tongue better than Clyde and Bonnie."

Penny presented her brilliant transatlantic smile, a rich reward that Jack would war and pillage to earn again. "It's not our time yet."

The stern waitress landed three glasses of red and a plate of shells on the white cloth. Jack snipped the ribbon, slurping the first mussel. Penny planted references to her Catholic conversion, taking place within the past year. The Roman apostolic tradition had undergone a resurgence in enthusiasm across downtown New York, verging on chic trend.

Out of the overhead speaker came a playlist of vintage sweet nothings, true love breathily exhaled 'til suns tumble out of skies and oceans freeze over and fish go extinct and nations grow hungry, all inexplicably wielding the word "baby" like an atomic weapon.

Jack excused himself to the toilette, leaning in line behind a woman with sharp French features, an ice queen who looked like an old LA fling fond of squirting buckets then clocking a 6am shift at a bagel shop. He looked back somewhat longingly at Penny, her healthy curves, round in the right places beneath those clothes, hinting at a cornfed rearing. He thought he'd end up with a frog, but after two false starts with la langue française, he felt drawn instead towards this fellow country bumpkin. Jack splashed sink water on his brow. His next few hands should be played with the utmost caution and a refusal to sacrifice routine for romance. Jack strolled back to their table and took a swig of wine, happy to fill the role of whimsical gentleman, regardless of outcome.

He overheard a lateral party discussing vaccines in hushed tones and adopted their thread of conversation. "Did you allow the mad doctor to give you a jab?"

"I was forced to, for work. It fucked up my period for like, nine months," Gwen said.

Penny made a cute retching noise. "That's a chemical pregnancy. Adam photoshopped a fake vax card for me. I'm interested in giving birth to non-retarded children someday."

Jack explained his own saga dodging government overreach: a hastily-edited stock image with cursive overlay, cooked up after four beers in a rented room in Odessa once he realized he needed medical paperwork to cross the border into Moldova. The poor approximation of experimental-poke proof permitted him entry into six additional countries until a German pharmacist fixed him up with an official EU printout, complete with QR code.

"The mark of the beast, times two," Penny added.

"My pretend docility looked more realistic than friends who actually took the plunge."

"What were you doing in the Ukraine?" Gwen asked, "Volunteer soldier?"

"This was before the invasion but after the annexation. I went to a forty-hour techno festival inside an active factory. I thought that region exported the most beautiful women in the world." Jack cut a side-eye towards Penny. "I was wrong." She giggled.

Gwen took their talk down a different tangent. "We should go dancing tonight."

"The vaccine didn't steal your sense of rhythm too?" They all laughed while he paid. "I know a decent spot nearby."

Jack led Penny and Gwen to a dimly-lit upscale yuppie bar, known for exclusively spinning disco hits. Last Halloween, Jack had grooved there with two other young gals he'd met while shooting billiards at a skater-cokehead bar in Bushwick. He had easily impressed the pair of undergrads with his ability to extract a hoot and a howl from the blockhead doorman, that towering Grendel of an ex-lineman who had kicked the girls to the curb the first time they attempted entry. Tough doors were a staggering deterrent to lames citywide who were unwilling to engage in choose-your-own-adventure chatter with the guards. With Penny and Gwen on either arm, Jack gained access once more to the ten-by-ten dance floor, edging out bouncing interns to clear the way for creative footwork. A former grunt in high-school drumline, Jack had spent four straight years training to never lose the beat. His lanky lower-half slid left and spun in jagged half-circles, hands refusing to remain glued to his sides, fingers stimming in the multi-colored refraction of the glitterball. Penny popped, locked, and dropped like a consummate professional on one hundred million TV sets for the halftime show, her same winsome smile uncracking atop the seamless flow of her body. She reminded him of a classic cartoon character, a sexpot rabbit or a sultry candy bar. Jack had rarely felt so aroused, so ravenous, so fast.

Gwen twirled, a German ballerina afraid of a beating, attracting the ogle of a bespectacled dandy with autobahn ambition. When four-eyes sidled past her to Penny, Jack stepped into the show, merging their movements without breaking stride, grasping her smooth palms, interlocking segments of a Vitruvian puzzle. He guided her three hundred and sixty degrees around and pulled her flush with his figure, almost daring her to point her toes and kiss him, then skipped backwards to return to the steady motion inspired by the turntables.

The song concluded with an earth-pummeling blast from the horn section. Jack and Penny joined Gwen and the random dork on the protruding lip of a heart-shaped water bed in the corner. The odd man out introduced himself as Lance, his affable nature—with an undercurrent of narcissism—explained by his aspiration to work as an actor. Encouraged by Gwen's fascination but directing his lines towards Penny, Lance held court like a tennis amateur, bumbling through an elevator pitch of his current project and shilling its cool factor by citing how the producer "could quote like any line from the dope-ass history of cinema." Bored wooden, Jack nudged Penny with his shoulder and rolled his eyes for her alone. He scribbled the line about movie quotes for later use. She reached for his pen and scrawled a note on a bar napkin: YOU'RE SO COOL :).

Penny checked her cell, a chunky flip. "My phone disappeared on a northbound train the second day in town, so I'm stuck with this junk."

Jack showed her his in return. "We're part of the same club, and you should be proud to be a member." He punched his digits into her device.

Penny placed her head on his shoulder and opened a recent text, displaying a deep-fried neon flyer with death-metal Swedish lettering, an offensive and impenetrable eyesore. "Some weirdo from that other event invited me here."

"If that says what I think it says then I know where that is."

The group progressed deeper into downtown. Penny and Gwen relished the opportunity to catch up and yap away. Jack avoided a one-on-one with Lance to eavesdrop on the girls, a simple assignment at half the volume, hearing Penny articulate some stained-glass vision of a holy site in SoHo, the ritual palatable enough to appeal to believers and skeptics alike, so consumed in her illumination that she almost crippled herself in oncoming traffic if not for Jack softly, firmly saving her soul with an arm across the chest.

"It'd be a shame to see you become a saint so soon."

The nondescript facade of a nineteenth century storefront obscured a two-tiered dreamscape that seemed much larger within, the main hall its own bifurcated venue resembling a former family home, wrought-iron balcony overlooking a gutted interior where the DJ manipulated his decks for normies fighting over a dwindling supply of serotonin. The basement housed a separate underworld: cyberpunk pageantry, bisexual lighting, a cryogenic vodka freezer and a legion of queers writhing in reckless excess.

Gwen and Lance, sucked in by the centrifugal force of golden oldies, remained upstairs to shake and sway while Jack and Penny descended into the pits below, fielding nasty looks from the alphabet horde as if they were shouting, "this is our domain, live dangerously all ye who enter here." The auditioning lovers tried their luck at dancing with a swag not suited for those surroundings, establishing a perimeter while zone denizens retreated deeper into the dark. A dirtbag photographer in an LA Kings flatbill positioned himself to snap an action shot of their hickety-har boogie, then disappeared into the crowd before the camera could flash.

Penny brushed her lips against Jack's ear to be heard over the ass-pounding bass. "Guess we didn't look gay enough."

Jack glanced down at his 'fit: acid-washed denim and a long-sleeve patterned with black and yellow diamonds. "Euro club kid up top, ghetto jobseeker underneath."

The downstairs disc-jockey more closely resembled a racehorse. He suddenly pulled the plug on the music in order to lecture at length, some hogwash repurposing the *Liberté-Egalité-Fraternité* of the French Revolution for Generation BLT.

Penny again leaned in close, her minty breath coating Jack's neck. "God instructs us to love everyone, but these people expect the *right* to live the *wrong* way."

Jack allowed his titillation to dominate his hesitation. "What are you doing tomorrow?"

"Well, you know I just moved to this big city and haven't seen the sights. I'm sure you've been plenty of times with other little birds...but won't you take me to Times Square?"

Towering jumbotron screens screamed in every dialect the great benefits of buy buy buy, digital prophets proclaiming the gospel according to ad-women and algorithms for a congregation of Chinese tourists assembled in the fourth estate's temple. At the end of history, the window between desire and fulfillment shrank to no time at all, contentmaxxing binges without the beauty treatment of a bulimic purge. Global Information Networks turned low-wage bonebags into servants: a husk to operate the selfie-stick spinning around each paying customer's personal center stage, producing prefab social posts to feed the hungry machine.

Penny stood tall, twice her height in attitude and spirit. "GET OUT OF MY HEAD!"

She looked to Jack, anticipating a laugh. He delivered, and then some. "DESTROY COMPUTER! DESTROY COMPUTER!"

Penny picked up the chant, a first-date initiation alienating stray passersby. They both smiled. She wore a red cape adorned with an iron cross, lunatic's toggery serving as mothlight for Mexicans hawking single roses for seven bucks a pop—and refusing to accept pesos! Jack took a dramatic knee to present her the flower. She sang a glorious and uplifting snippet from a folksy synth number about packing a pistol in an overnight bag before venturing north of 42nd St.

"Your impersonations got more talent than most people's genuine efforts." He mimicked Penny's country twang.

She beamed. "Thank you, Mr. Jack. I love to sing. I plan to be a pop-star."

"I plan to make you a pop-star, to turn the tide in this holy war."

He gestured at the promotional videos bathing their brainstorm, invoking a reference to religious history to align their goals in her mind. She took a whiff of the fresh rose.

He leaped up to grab the scaffolding, pumping out a dozen pull-ups to let the blood flow.

"Are you trying to impress me even more?"

Jack landed by her side, holding her cheeks with delirium. "Is it working?"

An hour split into two, temporal mitosis, and Jack had to skedaddle to an appointment at a hotel bar in Tribeca. The cost-benefit calculus—kissing a young gal before he was positive about his sentimental attachment, not to mention concern over spoiling the potential riches of pop-stardom with a rush-hour romance—came up negative, so Jack opted to part ways with sweet Penny sans smooch, body language from both shouting with reckless abandon for the polar opposite path. Delaying the inevitable felt proper, profound, a long-term plan conceived and executed. Jack was a half-decade beyond his sleazy era of cracking open the hearts of little girls, and the following week was too packed with activity to risk otherwise.

On Wednesday, Jack caught a screening of that prescient early-90s media satire: two infamous serial killers fall in love, kill fifty people, and win the hearts of the nation, yet the real psychopaths are the cop and the warden and the talking head on TV. The picture was unfairly awarded "Worst Film" by morons who slather spiced pork with table-salt and call their sisters lovers.

On Thursday, in a white-walled tomb of an apartment charging eighty fucking big ones at the callbox, Jack attended a DIY stageplay: a trite talkie, ten scenesters crammed on an ottoman, choking out dialogue penned by some grandstanding tin-eared wordsmith who paid ten grand for a featured interview in the *Times*.

Friday came and went with little fanfare outside of an instrumental introduction to Simone Richards, a commodities investor aiming to open a clubhouse for fringe political theorists in downtown Manhattan. She and Jack chummed it up over handguns and COINTELPRO at an Italian-themed party, inexplicably stuffed full of Japanese college students.

Penny texted him sporadic musings, hinting at a wish to tag along to anything at all on his calendar, but Jack's methods succeeded strictly within the parameters of independent operation, a style of conducting business which cringe newsletter gurus clumsily coined "solopreneurship." Most portmanteaus made him want to vomit; this one also gave him diarrhea. He called to debrief her about his neverending pursuit of the bag, the one with a money sign painted on the side in dull green.

"I went to Mass every evening this week, then barhopping each night, but I've been mostly well-behaved."

Jack paced back-and-forth on the sidewalk with his cell tucked between ear and shoulder. "Oh yeah? Did you confess your sins? Which ones?"

Penny chided him with a reminder that papal absolution was a private matter.

"I've sinned once or twice lately. Foul language..." He forced a dramatic pause. "...and lustful thoughts." He couldn't help himself; the inner dog always poked its snout out of the kennel.

Penny tittered at the other end of the line. "If you need arm candy for the masquerade tonight, I have fabulous costumes lying wrinkled in my suitcase."

"I'm privy to the ticket sales, we're already thirty people over capacity."

"But I'm so small! My thigh gap is back, I'll hardly take up any space at all."

"Next time. It's mainly boring speeches. Hope to see you before I leave for Berlin."

Jack caught a daredevil taxi to Battery Park City, finding a handful of volunteer-servants cleaning the rented venue: an art-nouveau ballroom with both coat check and talent green room on separate floors. The space between was reserved for one-eyed bartenders and pagan statues and extravagant pianos and secondary storage for winter wardrobe, plus a grand staircase and a large collection of busts depicting monarchs of various European lineage. Amante—a former Miss Universe, born in Colombia in the early nineteen hundred and eighties, now a wealthy widow, her late husband the type of man whose careless public sneeze wound its way into the high-society gossip column—wore a sheer silver number, sparkling in the candlelight, accentuating her enraged eyes. She screamed at Jack once he crossed the threshold.

"PUTA! There you are!"

Jack sauntered past an array of artistic objects to instead examine, with comic exaggeration, an empty black rack meant to hold deadstock postcards. He circled the functional item as if it belonged in the Louvre.

"Gee Amante, how much dough did this masterpiece run ya?"

The evening's headmistress gave a curt, cold laugh, signalling to the staff that they, too, could and should respond with glee. Since her husband "passed"—he had decamped to Normandy with a Boca Raton broad who had recently graduated from an all-girls Catholic high school, a topic forbidden to broach for those on payroll, and nearly everyone was—Amante had been drowning her abject loneliness with an esoteric passion project: denying the legitimacy of the Magna Carta, a thirteenth-century royal charter weaponized by seventeenth-century jurist Edward Coke as an argument against the divine right of kings. Niche academics lambasted the historical accuracy of Coke's position while recognizing it as a symbolic victory for representative democracy. Amante, a posh elitist despite her South American upbringing, stretched the case a step further, believing fervently that Coke's falsification in the name of the common man's legal freedom actually discredited the *entire* human rights movement, rendering any system of government outside of absolute monarchy fundamentally invalid and untenable. Yes, of course the election was stolen; all elections were stolen, from the deserving gloved hands of English royalty. No one quite understood her line of thinking, and no one cared: the coalition to repeal the Magna Carta toiled together under a large umbrella, attracting disillusioned Republicans and edgy cool kids and Fourth-Reich foot-soldiers and autocratic enthusiasts with Aspberger's, each faction aiming to use the others to seed their own particular brand of odious and confounding ideology. Zero percent of these groups credited Amante with spawning their shared subculture, so she organized this extravagant and expensive MAGA Carta Masquerade to cement her position as queen bee among the new-wave American aristocracy. She even stooped to selling print-on-demand merchandise emblazoned with bad nominative puns and worse graphic design—Edward Joke (gold "haha" clipart) and Edward Choke (WikiHow for Heimlich maneuver) and Edward Toke (baked, red-eyed Calvin & Hobbes) and Edward Broke (stock image search for "poor people")—plus plenty of actual coke stashed upstairs for the scene-fixtures and MFA students.

Night dawned, and the Battery Park banquet hall filled with in-the-know attendees and moderately curious plus-ones. Jack tapped his foot with increasing frequency, awaiting the arrival of his prominent journalist contact. Tuesday's dinner was spent cashing in a small favor that guaranteed the newspaperman's event attendance "on spec, no promises I can swing an editor on this goofy royal wedding." Monday's strategy meeting had ended with Amante's plastic-surgery mug spitting venom and bile when his answer to "how many reporters can we expect at this weekend's MAGA

Carta Masquerade" was presented on one semi-closed fist. Promotional efforts, as commanded, were focused on enlisting as many online right-wing personalities as possible, which tended to limit engagement from the legacy press. His warnings went unheeded by a spoiled adult woman accustomed to stacking cash for friends.

He spied a handful of goons building a renegade internet, a couple of homewreckers with a podcast detailing their extramarital liaisons, and a small army of self-styled "digital authors" who tweeted write-ups of their hard-partying jouissance, claiming to have their finger on the future's pulse in regards to journalistic immediacy—but no real reporters. A washed-up horse gambler, k-holing, bumped into Jack by the staircase. An internet magician performed Tarot readings for guests.

Jack wanted a card. "I'm going to Berlin for the next month. What should I expect?"

The mystic offered the deck, pulling The Fool. "Your life will permanently change."

Jack digested this news in a daze. He floated around the room, looking for the bylined writer, grabbing stares from the growing crowd for a questionable outfit choice: a two-piece suit dusted with rainbow glitter and a tiny t-shirt displaying an oversized automatic rifle. He had fielded plenty of homosexual intrigue—an ex-girlfriend had once even called him a "faggot"—but Jack's desires were situated comfortably along the straight-and-narrow.

With stomach-churning delay, the prominent journalist finally showed face. Jack pumped the man's hand twice. The evening's program began, and the first performer climbed the grand staircase to speak. This was an offbeat internet personality known as The Incrementalist, an ironic political caricature wearing an opaque guillotine hood who chewed the scenery about incremental social change, the need for checks and balances, the importance of federal bureaucracy, how democracy dies in darkness, blah blah blah, a sinking lecture littered with deep-cut cultural references and in-jokes for the tottering audience of extremely-online true believers to smirk at each other over, proud to be part of the king's court.

Amante ascended the steppèd stage next. Her thick Colombian accent, ever-present after multiple lazy decades stateside, was completely impenetrable to the average ear, even one of above-average snobbery. What little could be heard of her remarks bordered on ridiculous, praising moral truth and self-determination while her "dead" husband's coffers covered the evening's bill.

"This is the importance of establishing our own circuit of gatherings, places for open discourse catering to high-brow tastes, a moveable feast to dwarf the Met Gala and the Governor's Ball and the Whitney Biennial and the Correspondent's Dinner, not merely a party..." She droned on like this for some time, her audience composed of people simply looking for the next good party.

Polite applause carried her offstage. The mid-budget headliner arrived late from the back of a stretch limo with two e-girls on each obese arm. Gabriel Rosemont, the gay-baiting don of an alternative media organization, had made his bones blowing the whistle on the founder of a full-stack film empire, who happened to be the nephew of the grifter that popularized modern propaganda for politics and industry, who in turn happened to be the nephew of the father of institutional psychology and its many downstream armchairs. Implications of anti-goy brainwashing that targeted podunk, potato-chip-crunching stream-heads—the same demographic as, naturally, Gabriel's budding fanbase—ensured their outraged attention each Sunday when he dropped a fresh video report. There's an old saw about a joke, at the expense of powerful Jews, that offends Hollywood

Jews, who won't let the jokester perform 'til he apologizes, somewhat proving the merit of the material. Gabriel didn't bother making amends, plowing full-speed ahead into the depths of the dark web where his breaking news clips are still allowed to breathe. What any of this had to do with absolute monarchy, the best scryer in the business couldn't guess, but it served Amante's vision of giving the masquerade a "dangerous" edge. Gabriel had failed to maintain his health after the scandal, downshifting from good-looking golden-boy anchor to enormous and grotesque Ailes-Weinstein clone. The four e-girl attendants helped him mount each buckling step of the screaming wooden staircase in order to deliver his jowl-ish monologue.

"Esteemed gentlemen, beautiful ladies, I stand before you to discuss the significance of—" Mr. Rosemont discreetly, unsuccessfully, peered down at his pudgy hand. "—hierarchy."

Good Lord, it's a stunt casting, a minor name for the chocolate shell and duplicate Amante-brained talking points as the gooey filling.

"The natural world is built upon it. Think fondly of food chains, of photosynthesis."

This pompous oaf had a voice that boomed to the rafters yet absolutely nothing to say.

"Everyone learns in elementary school that birds of prey feast upon squirrels, if *they* even teach such *violent* rhetoric these days. But the social order of humanity has been inverted, with special-needs programs to help squirrels avoid their predestined fate as dinner."

Jack stood within reach of Mr. Rosemont, struggling to listen and make mincemeat meaning of this dictionary drumbeat. His poker face drifted towards the far wall, finding a discolored patch of paint that resembled a man beneath a boulder. Ah, the great myth of Sisyphus! Jack cracked a faint smile at the exact moment a camera flashed from the crowd, likely capturing him in frame with Gabriel. There goes the OPSEC neighborhood, blown away on a mild breeze. He was offline for a reason.

The zookeeper's problem child continued. "The only solution that tackles our decline in a comprehensive fashion is—" Another glance at the cue card inked on his fat mitt. "—absolute monarchy. Take my company as an example. Do you think we would be able to harpoon the neoliberal whales without a lone soul steering the ship? A council of halfwits giving input on each micro-decision would only stagnate the process, stalling our progress. I must have unilateral authority to call the shots, or I fear the entire operation might break apart into four-score and seven pieces."

The nod to Lincoln was baffling, but the rapt observers laughed all the same. Gabriel went on to propose an idiotic set of policies, then contradicted himself with a call for radical action, seizing the apparatus of power and installing a latter-day Caesar to reverse the effects of decay. The declaration earned thunderous applause from these delusional new-wave aristocrats, cornball fanfare disintegrating into a business-casual bacchanal with black-tie pretensions.

With all the hullabaloo, Jack dropped the ball on pinging Penny back the next day, sucked instead into a lamely organized response to the MAGA Carta contingent, a poetry reading gesturing at Frontier Horizons Of Antifascist Infowarfare Terminologies, according to the flyer, a word choice barely worse to choke down than the dozen long-winded demonstrations of mongoloid rhyme and meter themselves. The exclusive third floor of the Soviet bar was packed with effeminate beta males and the multicolored mullets of female masters. Jack recognized many familiar faces from the previous evening, scene-hoppers whose only allegiance belonged to their high-end coke dealers. Simone Richards reintroduced herself: a smokescreen bimbo stacking big bills, content to fund both sides of this ideological battle 'til one caved into controlled opposition. She made plans to meet more seriously with Jack over a game of billiards once he returned from Berlin.

The last "speech artivist" stood on a wooden platform, flanked by a bear and a twink decked out in leather kink gear, the two men providing X-rated pantomime while she read a story that somehow managed to link Ukrainian independence with the act of gay cruising. A hand-scrawled sign hung behind the performance area stated in clear terms that Clapping Is Colonialism, not that anyone would be moved to cheer on the randy exercise otherwise.

Patrons filed into the stairwell to get hammered in the larger room a floor below. Jack cornered a cute little thing to chat. "Did you bring your groceries to the function?" He indicated a pile of reusable totes by her feet, fair-trade snack boxes spilling out.

"Did you expect me to leave them behind at the supermarket?"

Snappy comeback; Jack was semi-charmed until the talk flipped into an explanation of her screenplay-in-progress, a crime caper in the vein of Capra that served to examine and interrogate her relationship with her gender identity. This chick was the epitome of normal girl next door, mind you. A growing sense of unease led him to wrongfully terminate himself from her conversational employ and head downstairs.

Alcoholic intake skipped once more, the bipolar decisioneer found solace with a homie at the corner of the bar, a green-gilled film producer exploring the option to remake Spike Lee's seminal early joint with a fully Caucasian cast: *Do the White Thing*. They gabbed for a couple minutes before Jack spotted a fuming slant-eyed glare: poor forgotten Penny, with Gwen in tow. The reunited trio commandeered a table and hunkered down to brass tacks.

"How was your lousy masquerade?"

"Unapologetically awesome."

Penny punished her nerves, flaying skin from her thumb and holding it over the candle.

"Quit with the self-mutilation." Jack kissed her delicate fingers.

"Don't fucking play games with my best friend's heart, you bastard," Gwen said.

"The hell is your problem? I had a busy week."

His defensive reaction ran its course after he explained the trials of the previous eight days. Penny boldly, intensely scratched his scalp with her three-chord grip, transforming excuses into mild whimpers of bliss. A scrap of receipt paper caught fire on the open flame, and the methhead bartender watched him quickly and safely extinguish the threat, still screaming about how he "COULD HAVE KILLED EVERYONE IN HERE, YOU KNOW THIRD DEGREE BURNS ARE NO LAUGH, GET THE FUCK OUTTA MY BAR!"

Jack and company, failing to stave off a case of the giggles, obeyed her loud orders. The remaining drinkers clapped and cheered.

"We had to preserve the blaze of our ancestors, even at the risk of exile from the cave."

A drunk Penny leaned into Jack's chest, and he slid an arm around her little waist. They stumbled against the dim glow of a Bank of America ATM. Gwen walked away into the night.

Penny held Jack close to her face. "I skipped all the way home after you gave me that flower. You sure cast a spell over this feral girl." She shifted into a white trash twang. "Won't you be mine, Jack Valentine?"

"I'm off to Europe for a month and you just got to town, don't you want to—"

"I wrote a song about what I want. I want to stick my tongue between that adorable gap in your two front teeth."

She sang him a private melody, lyrics nodding to their chance meeting and brief first date. Jack revealed his apparently revered gap-toothed grin. Penny grabbed the lapels of his coat and pulled him into their sloppy and delicious star-spangled first kiss, an extensive and experimental block of boundless passion, the wet stuff of legend.

Penny whispered into his ear. "I'd love nothing more than to destroy your routine."

And so she did, terraforming his final week in the nation with every-other-evening hangouts, beginning with a pained excursion to a friend's acting workshop for a public showcase from the new class of students. Most of the scenes were deeply-underlined sob stories about AIDS, a trend that Jack tallied on Penny's exposed thigh with sharpie, silly boy behavior encouraged by her voracious laughter.

A trifecta of thieves thick with impudence invaded the stage. The narrator fulfilled her duty while leather-clad assistants groped each other, in sync with the tall tale.

Jack groaned. "I can't believe I have to sit through this bullshit a second time."

"*Do you like to party?*" The narrator's back-up actors mouthed the dialogue perfectly.

"This little five-word code phrase never fails to secure a bag of crystal stateside, so Jonathan Bean—thinking his bachelor's in street linguistics applies outside the continental forty-eight—assumes an easy one-to-one translation here in the dim, dark corner of Anastasia's, a popular discothèque and pick-up bar in eastern Kiev. He spies a decent target across the room: a stern Slav with a clenched jaw, appearing in vermilion glow of spotlight scanning pulsing bodies near DJ booth. The thudding four-on-the-floor bass hits of hard techno provide the score for Jonathan's footsteps while he saunters towards the mark, a dopamine dealer by any other name. His first request goes unheard. His second, unacknowledged. His third, shrieked at a high-enough register to turn the heads of a half-dozen nearby party-likers, earns the Goldilocks treatment, the volume just right to flag the attention of the muscle-bound wife-beater grinding his teeth to the beat. *You want party, no?* Jonathan hears this bit of broken English as music to his ears."

The narrator paused for the cheap laugh.

"The hulking merchant darts his bloodshot peepers left, right, up, down—then gestures for Jonathan to follow him upstairs to the fleet of stalls, a place of glorious excess liberated from the shame of sunlight. Tucked away inside the porcelain chamber, Jonathan digs in his pocket for keys to sample the goods, plus cash—*hryvnia*, in local parlance— to seal the deal. His companion motions for Jonathan to turn around. Highly sensitive to minute cultural differences and seeking to avoid a quandary, Jonathan obeys, averting his gaze to the tune of a belt buckle unclasping. He finds his own pair of parachute pants falling to the ground and a stiff intruder brushing up against his rear. He ponders this new method of payment. Highly sensitive to minute cultural differences and seeking to avoid a quandary, Jonathan allows the buff stranger to fuck him in the ass."

The two assistants wrapped up the sodomite's charade and took a bow. The audience applauded for their thespian bravery. Penny voiced the only review needed: "Gross."

The material had warmed up well after a repeat viewing, and he never turned down an opportunity to countersignal, so Jack explained how he thought the twee mannerisms were meant to make a mockery of international relations.

"That makes you the biggest retard in the room," Penny cooed, rubbing her nose on his.

She dragged him to another scene-party-80s-music-bar-hang forwarded to her via text-chain, finding a club with deserted dance floor but plenty of vibrant sofas 'round the perimeter. Penny and Jack naturally chose a love-seat for their delightfully sober heart-to-heart, sharing personal anecdotes and partial amusements as if they alone were granted the privilege of existing.

Penny described her wayward path to conversion, from a cursory interest in chaos magic—dead bugs and hair follicles repurposed for living room rituals—to a spiritual awakening, six months of classes on the process of belief and a five-hour graduation, entirely in Latin, on Easter Sunday, surrounded by both blood relatives and chosen Catholic family.

"I ran away from cohabitation with my freak of an ex and nearly had a three-way with an incel and a pregnant teenager. Slouching towards God was anything but linear."

Jack felt shoved in the lower gut. He despised thinking of her laid out naked at the mercy of another man, on her back or hunched down like a dog, legs spread, some schmuck gripping her body. Even offhand details found a way to hijack his brain and fill it with dirty images, a crippling debt owed to fifteen years of obsessive-compulsive porn consumption.

"Last year I got a little carried away with the girlies, an easy lay to waste the day away, 'til I sobered up and realized all that sex was a critical drain on my supreme levels of vitality."

A castle brat, demanding that mother send away the concubines so he could practice archery.

Penny laughed. "That must mean you're Mr. Vitality now. How many months celibate?"

"Three." An honest answer. "You?"

She stroked her chin in jest. "How many days are in this month? Kidding. I stopped counting after twelve. Twelve months."

Penny excused herself to the restroom, and Jack fixated on the threesome remark. He had initiated many, the first with Violet—they met at a house party through mutual British accents—and Hazel—they met when she was still a high school photo assistant—after a shimmering road trip to find and claim a haunted house on Cumulonimbus Lane, one suitcase full of books and one full of warm beer, one girl with her ass in the air and one moaning like a dripping-tap wraith, the pair having their way with each other while he observed from a mounted position, but neither had been pregnant, it was an experience missing from his mostly comprehensive yet incomplete bank of—

"Let's hear another memory, no debauchery this time," Penny said.

Jack reminisced about four pious strongmen who had visited his primary school in order to crack wood with their skulls, recline on a bed of nails, walk on swords, and swallow hot coals. Upon insistent urging, his parents had taken him to a follow-up performance in the basement of a church, where he learned that these devil-may-care feats were powered by Jesus Christ himself; when the time came to accept that Protestant version as his Lord and Savior, Jack leapt to his feet and sprinted for the altar.

Penny replaced him in the story seat, an exchange of fragmented history spanning multiple days and environments, the next a different corner couch in a renovated hotel in Chelsea that used to trade rent for paintings or services, a place of tantric power immortalized by that horny Canadian poet who sang of getting dome on messy beds.

"You kept me waiting for more than a week. I was a Jack fanatic. Gwen called it the Eight Day Itch." Penny lounged with a second glass of red in her hand.

"Part of any man's effective strategy. Put 'em on ice for a little spell. Didn't it work?"

She beamed, and he took the chance to shift a short staring contest into a public makeout session, their tastebuds all mixed together for a glorious sixty seconds straight.

Jack leaned back into the cushions. "How much junk did you lug to the big city?"

"A trunk full of clothes, a backpack for makeup and prayer tracts, and a banjo that needs restringing. The rest of my possessions are stashed across Ohio, including a small but obscure record collection at my mom's house."

"Is your dad still around?"

"He found new kids to support. You know that cheesy Christmas song where the guy bumps into an old flame in a supermarket and they knock back a few cold ones and wax nostalgic about the ancient past before parting ways in the rain? That's my father, except his story had a happy ending."

"Your dad is Dan Fogelberg?"

"My dad might as well be Foghorn Leghorn. Mom raised us up from the dirt."

Jack let the news sink in, mind drifting to the electric streets he'd soon leave behind. He caressed Penny's face.

"Don't worry, I won't abandon you for my second family in Berlin."

She laughed. "I don't have daddy issues! And this is your last evening in town, not a therapy session."

"It's in the blood. My mom is a psychologist. Each birthday gift was a fresh diagnosis."

"I almost forgot my duty as a young woman in the internet age. When were you born?"

"I used to resent this part, 'til my interests grew more esoteric. A Catholic and a magic-man walk into a bar—" He smooched a different spot on her cheeks between each letter: "—K-I-S-S-I-N-G...R?"

"You are crazy! When's your birthday?"

"Pisces sun, Gemini moon, Leo rising."

"I'm a Pisces too." Penny glanced across the lobby to a mirror, puckered her lips and fixed her hair. "The stars indicate you're quite the playboy."

"You're meeting me in my evolved state."

They stumbled into the frigid darkness near midnight, the wounds from Cupid's arrows disinfected by the devil's juice.

"Two two-fish-in-water in love, two fish—fuck. Try that ten times fast."

A flirtatious, shocked look on her face. "You mustn't say these things!"

"Are you serious? I've loved you from the minute I laid eyes on you. Come home with me, I want to sleep with you before I go. Next to you. Chaste, fully-clothed, no funny business."

Penny pulled away, eyes peeled for a taxi. "I told my mom I wouldn't kiss a man before marriage. She didn't believe me. How many rules are you going to encourage me to break?"

A rare gift: not a yellow cab in sight. Jack held her hand. "I promise I won't force myself on you. Even if it would give you something else to put in a song."

Penny buried her face in his coat, giggling. "If anyone asks about this later, I'm saying that I was kidnapped by a Hell's Kitchen warlock."

They spent twenty minutes waiting for the uptown train, locked in a single, delicate kiss. "Practice makes perfect."

Penny relaxed on the bed while Jack tightly rolled his closet of odd shirts, fitting them neatly in his single suitcase.

"I feel like I'm watching a nature documentary on boys."

Jack gifted her a pack of childish stickers bearing his name, balloons and hearts and rabbits and automobiles.

"I've had these for almost two decades. Mostly unused. Put them all over town while I'm away."

Penny held the booklet to her bosom. "You mean put them all over my room?"

He also uncovered a nearly-empty bag of ketamine, too risky for travel. "It's our duty to sniff through the rest of this."

Penny sighed. "My next confession grows longer by the minute."

They took turns exploring the art of the key bump, a fine line Jack always managed to cross into a fully-tranquilized state. He laid in the warmth of her arms, drifting from a dissociative state towards slumber. Penny played soft ballads from the scratchy speaker on her flip phone, a track by one of those Warhol Factory guys, something about falling in love with a girl who goes to Amsterdam and fucks somebody else.

The budding couple bid adieu to that Hell's Kitchen apartment for good, and each other for the span of the year's shortest, coldest month. Jack departed for the ill-advised Jersey-side airport without fear of the future or needless pain from the past, embracing instead a complete and total peace in the moment, his heart inscribed with the fancy signature of one Penny Delphine. A string of texts arrived while he progressed through buses and security checkpoints to his gate.

I held you all night in your infantile k-hole.

His boarding group shuffled into line.

It's nice to be able to wreak havoc in such a short amount of time.

He found his seat, the economy section. One final, foreboding statement stood tall like a tower missing its twin, the boon of a brief prologue in this city that shimmers above the sand, the land of heroin chicks and heroines chic, undergrounds lined with velvet and infested with rats.

I think I might have Stockholm Syndrome.

2
Mitte

"If it's good P.R., see that it's P.'d."

— David Foster Wallace

On his first two journeys to the center of German power, Jack had found fast friendship from locals and fleeting, sexual intimacy with expats, indulging in booze and ecstasy and yerba mate to traverse the club scene by night, then kill time in climate-controlled botanical gardens during the day. On this trip, the city itself seemed to repel his presence. A conversation, overheard in the customs line, on the relative safety of the European landmass compared to the "glut" of school shooters stateside, spelled certain doom for his travels when interpreted through the looking glass of hindsight, cleaned with the microfiber cloth of irony.

Jack woke with fright in his borrowed one-bedroom apartment, a pool of sweat staining the sheets, a searing memory from the night before looping behind his eyes. A jaunt to the oldest cinema in Berlin had gone awry after he was nearly stabbed to death, in the metro station, by a man strung out on hopes and prayers. The Arab brandished a knife and stole his thin gold-flake necklace, simple costume jewelry. Jack's desires shifted from safe escape to the visceral need to snap the thief's neck, in full view of his *khalīfah*, summoning a blood-oath fatwa. Molten visions of a future unfulfilled: reactionary tabloids decried the death of an Aryan tourist at the hands of an immigrant. Memetic images of icon destruction featured captions like IMPORT THE THIRD WORLD, BECOME THE THIRD WORLD. Surrealist activists planned to remix the message, chopped and fried visuals of post-human superhighways, rendered as nasty blood clots with the label FIFTH WORLD PROBLEMS in bold red comic sans. Jack's younger brothers also prospered from bright blonde hair and pale blue eyes, kinfolk ripe for radicalization if that subway shuffle went sideways, a blunt blade in the gut like a latter-day Gavrilo Princip, set to hard launch one thousand years of *Race Wars* (streaming this fall on Disney Plus). Even the most visible surface area of the video-on-demand labyrinth played host to burq'd-up shawties, oppressed beauties used as reliable recruiting tools for fundamentalist Islam, targeting the easily-aroused young men of the information age. The progeny of western civilization were no different, falling prey to pussy subsidized by the military-industrial complex, patriotic broads lip-syncing to Sousa in camouflage fatigues while squeezing landmines between their large breasts. Jack reserved the worst judgement for his own affairs, finding himself wrapped around the guitar-girl fingers of a CIA-sponsored succubus, just a total data-collection honeypot type job—and he fell for it, head slapping heels, never once doubting that a girl so perfectly tailored to his tastes as to seem constructed in a garment factory could be anything except organically interested in his secret hobbies and private pursuits of street-level justice. This unknowing affiliation with the engorged apparatus of American spycraft brought him under the strict surveillance of Stasi agents involved in some forty-year feud before coming in from the cold, complicating the assigned mission here in Berlin: a wheatpaste blitzkrieg, depictions of the false prophet Muhammad designed to incite an uprising in this abandoned imperial capital, relinquishing another stronghold of ancient power to men with explosive eyes and virgin brides. The ideological disposition of the entity validating the chèques remained to be seen.

Melatonin hallucinations don't pay the bills; Jack needed to vacuum the red carpet before Amante's imminent arrival. The move across time zones had knocked him nocturnal, and there were crucial emails to schedule for the following New York morning. His true task here was simple—simply-stated, but a bitch and some change to execute. Each February, thousands of industry professionals and a handbasket of hopefuls descended on Berlin, like an invading horde of world-music warriors and battle-hardened beatboxers, for

Eur-808: a tradeshow and songwriting showcase intended to demonstrate the breadth of national business opportunities available inside the European Union. An armada of producers and singers from America, Britain, Botswana, Argentina, and elsewhere attended as well, to peruse bleeding-edge amplification technology and score lucrative record deals in niche global markets, usually by organizing ten-grand talent shows in hotel conference rooms and inviting enough boutique label A&R reps to fill a few dozen office chairs until one or two well-dressed but shaggy fish decided to take a nibble. Jack had selected over a hundred worthwhile targets to gently encourage or bribe into appearing at Amante's scheduled, invoiced performance: a six-minute sample of an opera she had composed about the Magna Carta, featuring background dancers dressed as medieval peasants and four-bar female falsetto sure to shatter several complementary water glasses.

"It's not opera, it's cabaret, and we'll be laughed back to the east coast for insisting otherwise." Jack had presented this argument during one of her sporadic good moods.

"I'm not paying you for your ideas."

So Jack appeased her delusions and included language like "avant-garde operatic homage" in his outreach, digging through a list of distributors based in the UK, the birthplace of that infernal royal charter; the shared cultural heritage couldn't hurt, and at least they spoke English. He also emailed the obligatory set of international journalists with press passes, hoping to land a few articles as evidence of rent, food, and airfare not entirely gone to waste. Optimistic rumors circled the conference like crows, whispers of scouts for the Eurovision Song Contest haunting hotel bars near the convention center, occasionally popping their coiffed heads into the various showrooms in pursuit of the next Yves Dessca.

With Eur-808 slated to commence in five days and Amante's plane arriving in four (three, two, one…haha, not really), Jack cracked his knuckles and clocked a shift in his inbox, pasting the same boilerplate copy ad infinitum and tweaking opening lines to add the illusion of personalization. Satisfied after a job half-done, he closed his laptop and ventured around his sleepy mid-city neighborhood on foot; his brush with Crusade violence had scared him out of riding the rails, even if the Berlin metro lacked turnstiles or attendants and was therefore a foreigner's gratuity. He stumbled upon a trendy late-night café, Parisian-style, a place to sip cheap Sternburg Export and debate comrades on the merits of Communism according to Marx, Mao, Lenin, Stalin, and Pol Pot. A lonely arriviste, and an avowed anti-Red like his cursèd Camelot namesake, Jack settled for the beer and the view: geriatric men vying for the eye of a young gal sitting solo and sketching, their untranslated May-December pick-up racket likely amounting to nothing more than, "hows about you draw a picture of me, sweetheart," the oldhead equivalent of "where my hug at" saps.

On a trudge across town in the next day's light, Jack passed a pretty nice set-up for a bum: a concrete inlet occupied by stacks of textbooks, decorative lemon and lilac umbrellas to protect against rain, and a bed in the middle, topped with so many down comforters that he swore the guy was Inuit. The lifestyle tableau seemed staged, a first-draft thesis from a fine-art education. Jack theorized as much at an early dinner with Luke and Judy Moore, a mid-50s couple who had emigrated from Oregon twenty years prior. Judy was a high-school friend of his therapist mother, and boy would Mrs. Valentine have her legal pad full with this husband and wife on the chaise longue. They dug into three tender prime ribs and Luke cast the first stone.

"Another package came for you today. That's the second this week. We might have to move to a flat with more square footage if this pace continues."

Luke wore dreadlocks, from salad days playing in the Pacific Northwest's most tolerable reggae group. Jack turned to Judy, waiting for that Wimbledon serve to be returned.

"Do you remember all those boxes that came last month? Bearing your name? I considered shopping for a storage unit."

"You were probably browsing for that shit already." Luke swiveled to include Jack, an unsolicited act of kindness. "She's addicted to buying things online." He repeated it to her face. "You're addicted to buying things online. And those were replacement drum heads for my kit, that counts as one."

"Check my purchase history! Right now! It's mainly gifts for you!"

"Yeah, junk that we have to find shelf space to display, Chinese trinkets that wither under light scrutiny. Your generosity knows no bounds."

Judy stared into her soup, a delicious cream-of-broccoli prepared as the perfect side dish for the ribs. Luke compulsively checked football stats. Judy tried her hand at virtual slots. Jack waited the appropriate half-hour, post-meal, before departing for home, a balance sheet full of "thank you so much, we'll have to do this again sometime" lying in his wake.

Back at the short-term rental, he booted up his computer and found a pleasant surprise: the first email in what could be an ongoing exchange while he was MIA from NYC, subject line reading REQUIEM FOR UNCLE K and reply-to address starting with penny_delphine_music@.

My dear Jack, I hope this note finds you settled into your temporary shelter in Berlin. Since you're in my corner now, you have unlocked exclusive access to unreleased material. This is a song I wrote and recorded after a tumultuous evening wallowing in the depths of a mushroom trip. My first and final experience tasting the devil's shit! I think you will appreciate the message. Glad to meet a fellow soldier in this holy war. I keep praying for your safe return. Je ne veux pas me laver, Je veux rester couverte de tes baisers. From the heart, Penny.

Attached to the email was a low-megapixel snap of one of his Jack-stickers stuck to her elegant, swan-like neck. Appended below the typed message was a hyperlink leading to an unlisted track. He clicked play, and the haunting hum of a synthesizer chord pierced the tapestry of his insomnia. What followed was a slow-paced funereal dirge, a lament for the soul of Ted Kaczynski, with Penny's powerful bellow announcing that his stance against industrialized society may have been the correct choice. Five minutes passed, a poignant eternity. Jack's skin swarmed with gooseflesh. He wrote back a kind message, complimenting her musical revolt against the ripe stench of modernity.

Later, Jack tossed and turned, the victim of pernicious jet-lag. Berlin night life ran rampant on the outskirts of residential zones, noise contained by concrete borders, sound-proofed to maintain discretion, leaving his 'hood of Mitte—literally "center"—as the peaceful *herz von hurrikan.* Despite the solitude, there was nary a sheep in sight, so Jack climbed from the oddly slim trundle bed and illuminated the space with harrowing overhead light. The flat was an Ikea sanitarium, the hue from ceiling to floor matching the appliances and furniture and decor, every surface a kind of door, opaque interiors blocked from view, limiting access from them to you, a rootless cosmopolitan rental market, tubes for pet vermin to funnel between continents without obligation to engage culturally with the new environment.

The brazen gurgle of the toilet at twice the typical decibels drew his awareness to the bathroom, the sound of a wasteland creature crawling from farm to table. Jack walked to investigate, finding nothing but a stupid sticky note from the homeowner reading PLEASE WIPE DOWN WALLS AFTER EACH SHOWER :).

Jack curled up on the living room couch—same color palette, etc.—with a thick tome documenting the history of active measures: state-sanctioned campaigns of disinformation, aimed on occasion at enemy populations but usually targeting their own. Not a soul would flock to the Magna Carta Cabaret unless given quite a nudge, so Jack was brushing up on time-tested techniques of trickery. He looked forward to hosting Ezekiel, who planned to crash on this very sofa for the duration of the conference, lending his strategist's hat for use in their one-bed war room.

A light knock tip-tapped at his deadbolted door. Through the peephole, Jack observed a short girl in paisley camo looking lost on the fourth-floor hall, her distant familiarity scratching at the base of his brain like a tumor. He opened the door cautiously; she seemed vaguely Russian, and Jack was hip to all the latest snatch 'n' grab tactics in use by vodka-swilling special officers and their post-Romanov romantic lures.

"Can I help you?" he said, squinting at the woman, not bothering to stumble through the greeting in German.

"Fuck off Jackie, I've been traveling all day, let me sit down before starting with the clown routine," she replied, the faint trace of a Slavic tone gracing her tongue.

She pushed past him into the apartment, tossed her bag on the couch, and snooped around the kitchenette for something to whet her whistle. The black box guarding his memory began to fade, revealing the spectral presence in his home to be something far more fully-realized than a sleepless night's mirage.

"Katya?"

The woman whipped around, her hair a bottle-blond cat-o-nine-tails ready to lash him for his insolence.

"There's water with gas in the mini-fridge."

Use the phrase "sparkling water" on a European and watch their confidence in your sanity disappear. Precious jewels sparkled, drinking water was gaseous. Jack had learned the distinction on his first trip to Berlin some four-odd years ago, during the same excursion when he met Katya, swiping right on her profile after recognizing the Milan Kundera reference in her bio: "a woman of laughter and forgetting." His flowering fixation on the great Czech author had stemmed from an abandoned collaborative hip-hop mixtape adapting chapters from that book on ontology, unbearable lightness and being and nothingness, or whatever. The stretch goal had involved a flight to Paris to convince the famously reclusive novelist to record a spoken-word intro for one of the tracks, but the project never materialized due to the producer's greed.

Jack's first date with Katya, however, did indeed. She met him in the dark near a metro station, wearing sheer leggings and white fur, a potential victim of sex trafficking, a prostitute planning to solicit him for cash after a few hours of intellectual conversation and mild banter, the Kundera reference an obvious plant based on close monitoring of imprisoned thoughts inside his skull. She was smart and feisty and opinionated and didn't charge him for the lay. They fornicated quickly in her nearby friend's "spare bedroom": a broom closet with a mattress on the floor, firmsides pushing against the walls like voluptuous flesh overflowing from a corset. After some misplaced erotic energy—a sensuo-transactional sidetrack, one (1) forty-euro handie from a genuine lady of the night punctuated by bucktoothed, broken-English upsells with his meat at full mast—Jack invited himself to stay at Katya's apartment out in the suburbs. He transported his suitcase, adjusted his return flight, and decided to ride the fling to its dramatic conclusion instead of withdrawing with a timed detonator of later regret. They smoked cigarettes out of her kitchen window and acted like Russian grandmothers, watching the streets below for material to churn the gossip mill, where every guy is a hood and every gal is a whore. They stole a shopping buggy to cart back thirty liters of beer, pounded over the course of four nights. Katya enjoyed getting choked 'til she was unconscious and having her thighs bruised with the thunder of closed-fist American punches, an unspoken BDSM contract inked in bodily fluids on International Women's Day. The second time he came to Berlin, she had already returned to Novosibirsk, her tutoring gigs hitting a dry spell. Jack's checking account for once was flooded, and he paid for her Tran-Siberian train so that she could join him for another sexscapade. She was a mail-order bride, all of the bills and none of the commitment. They romped through perverse art galleries and rolled on MDMA in sushi bars and danced mechanically at krautrock concerts and cut demos with a vocoder and, yes, he laid his pipe into her like war was on the horizon. Her country invaded its former territory a few months later, and Jack lost contact. Their bond had been resurrected while making arrangements for this year's Eur-808, much to his present confusion and chagrin. Falling for Penny had sandblasted these pre-determined plans for sex-tourism from his mind.

Katya crashed in his bed; that small strip of cushioned white beside her sprawled form seemed unappealing, even if his desires were raging. He caught some shut-eye on the sofa. The clanging of cast-iron pans annihilated his third REM cycle, and the HVAC unit sparking to life precluded further rest, sounding as it did like a sewing machine or an unsynced 16mm camera.

"Want breakfast, valentine?"

Never before had she referred to him with the brusque shorthand of a football coach. He checked the stamp-sized screen on his flip: Feb. 14th, feast day of one St. Valentine, his other namesake, patron of Hallmark cards and body chocolate and overpriced dinner reservations.

"I'll take eggs and toast while you're in there."

Sleep had stalled her eternal diatribe, and he'd landed inside a weekend staycation for lovers. He needed to nip this in the bud. Nip... breasts... bud... weed... Jack was delirious. Katya brought two plates of hard yolks and burnt bread to the couch and gave him a stiff kiss.

"Sorry to behave like a typhoon at the front door last night. Why didn't you sleep next to me? I was cold."

Jack moved his slop from side to side with a fork. "You're from Siberia, your body has adapted for worse weather. And look at that bed, then look at me."

Katya laughed. "You are a gentle giant."

They silently choked down the food she had cooked. Two heads, separate clouds. He checked his email while she washed the dishes.

"You are a stern old man, hard at work, and I am a wife, cooking and cleaning." Katya leaned over the counter to kiss his cheek. "And loving."

Before parting ways on the last occasion, Jack had told her that he loved her and didn't "care how demented that sounds," an admission growing sour in the carton.

"Let's go for a walk, shall we?"

They strolled from district to district, bathed in the late-afternoon light.

"How have you been since the invasion?"

Katya supplied the details of a life utterly unknown to him, a refugee in every way minus official status, hiding among a population hostile to the fatherland of bears and ice. They walked past a pack of derelicts, barking like dogs at objects crossing their cones of vision, resetting a minute later, beholden to the game's code. Katya, startled from her story, cursed at them in Russian.

"*Vam nuzhen Bog, ublyudki!*" She clasped a hand over her mouth, brow furrowed, face colorless. "I must not do that here. When Ukrainians hear the language of oppressors, they have great anger. Sometimes they make street violence."

Back home, Katya grabbed Jack's open palm, an act of light eros that he reluctantly allowed. She wanted to watch a specific movie, so he pirated and played her on-the-nose choice, some MP4 romcom about an American student swooning over a French seductress on a train, their courtship lasting only until sunrise the following morning and failing to end on the floor of a hostel bathroom stall. Midway through the film, Katya straddled Jack's lap, grinding firmly, forcing him to grow taut as rebar.

"Can we make sex?"

Her broken plea overwhelmed his defenses, and he yanked up her shirt to place his wet mouth around her nipple. She responded in kind, tugging at the torqued appendage between his legs. Jack dropped both their jeans and slid himself across her warm thighs, hesitating to penetrate. A man of sharp timing, he chose that moment to unveil his evolving situation.

"I almost have a girlfriend now."

Katya sucked his neck. "I've had a boyfriend for five years, that never stopped us before."

Jack neared the gaping prize then snapped to his senses. "I can't do this, I'm sorry."

At any other point in his adulthood, Jack would have shagged her senseless, but now he had a streak of chastity to uphold, and a dime named Penny waiting for him across the ocean, in his real life. To the tune of Katya's moaning complaints, Jack retired to the bedroom alone to masturbate, his desires conquered, satiated by a fleeting solution.

Jack shuffled his reformed tsarina out the door the next morning, pockets full of pity petty cash so that she could book a room elsewhere. Her whining goodbye flagged the attention of Ezekiel, who arrived at the exact same moment, ready to ride Jack's coattails through the music industry marketplace.

"Who was that ear of buttered corn?"

Zeke always had some new expression to trot out, slang for women or ways of describing music, words swirling 'round his throat before being put on trial, often let off the hook by a jury of peers.

"What are you doing here? The conference doesn't start 'til Saturday."

Ezekiel dragged his rollerbag and tuxedo sleeve past Jack into the flat, taking stock of the amenities, a freeloader's paradise.

"My boy, today is Friday, which makes the day in question tomorrow. What fool flies overnight without a solid twenty-four to adjust before a big money-making opportunity? Now, where's my bed?"

Jack gestured towards the couch, which Katya had disassembled into a pullout—some cryptic message afoot there—and logged into his email, finding positive RSVPs for the Magna Carta Cabaret from contacts with names like Stanislav and Volodya and Ivanovsky. He consulted the Eur-808 online directory, coming to grips with his colossal blunder.

"Fuck me running."

"That's good, where'd you pick it up?" Zeke chimed in from the sofa bed.

"Card games with the Gay Mafia."

For some mystifying reason, the organizers of this godforsaken conference of clerical errors had chosen to classify

England with the country code GB, for Great Britain, leaving UK as the signifier for Ukraine. In his somnambulist's haste, Jack had forwarded several dozen invitations to the wrong non-members of the European Union. Maybe there would be perks, limited competition for deals or political association with a freshly sacred cow. His salesman's brain whirred to life, searching for angles. It was too late to course-correct; the British inboxes were sure to be drowned or ignored this close to kickoff. A new message pinged, this one from its.just.amante@.

EMAILING FROM PLANE YOU BETTER NOT BE GOOFING OFF PUTA MEET ME FOR DINNER LATER HERE.

A map-app hyperlink appended below the note also suffered from a disordered grasp of caps-lock.

"I've made a huge mistake," Jack admitted, phone tucked between head and shoulders. He and Ezekiel chain-smoked outside a massive brutalist cube with tight security. Ex-patrons stepped through the revolving doors, dressed to the nines, their meals finished, their private carriages idling in the valet crescent near the street.

"You always seem to land on your feet," Penny said.

"This weekend abounds with possibility. Might not have that many chances to talk. I miss you something fierce."

Penny shared a story of a recent romp through the night, dodging the desperate claws of dark simps content to neg for an hour straight before trying to cop a feel. Jack promised to enact sharia law upon his return: the next man who tried to touch her would lose his hand in a ceremony attended by the entire social scene, and the mutilation would be branded as performance art.

Jack hung up and recounted his Manhattan tryst for Zeke, highlighting the detail about Penny's celestial songwriting abilities.

"Nice, nice. So that Russian chick fleeing your flat was only the maid?"

For an impresario who prided himself on his spotless record of tastemaking, Zeke was often shortsighted when the scent of fresh blood wafted under his nostrils.

A black limo deposited Amante and her flowing red dress on the curb. She cursed the driver in Spanish and strutted to the entrance, awareness buried in her phone for a string of minutes before she finally looked up, *con una sonrisa diabólica.*

"I had to file an incident report. That motherfucker didn't even thank me as I left the vehicle!"

Amante kissed Ezekiel on both cheeks, fancying herself French for the evening, then squinted at Jack. The trio proceeded inside, an opulent members-only club awaiting them just beyond the check-in booth. From the grand foyer, Jack looked up, the open floor plan revealing ten mezzanines protruding in the direction of an obsidian chandelier. Every level held hidden goods and services, a kickboxing gym and a semi-nude spa and a restaurant with bioluminescent food lit solely by blacklight. Both staff and visitors contributed to the Venkateswara atmosphere, dispensing warm smiles and banal pleasantries. The path from the building's grey exterior to its decadent guts was jarring in its antipodal quality, suggesting a lair for villainy.

"Gee Amante, how'd you dig up this hole-in-the-wall?"

"My ex-husband was a majority shareholder. Let's eat, shall we?"

She ordered for the table, Chinese style, an assortment of small plates, Spanish style, winking at Zeke after each selected item was introduced by the waiter, who announced at the top that the dishes would be delivered once they were prepared, as if this distinguished the eatery from others in any tax bracket. Jack thought his two mid-40s dining companions had met before, but soon realized that this wasn't the case when Zeke launched into his spiel, The Rise and Fall of an Independent Music Magnate. Amante paid close and careful attention to the lovable windbag's every exhale; she even provided shocked gasps during the most dramatic story beats. Jack was thankful to have brought such a loquacious guest, whose mere turnkey tales thrilled, perhaps even titillated, Amante. Was the bitch in heat?

Servers in animal masks carried platters of pre-made cocktails for quick grab 'n' go sips of pleasure. A man in white ninja garb sliced up sushi with a katana, the fish bits ferried from party to seated party on a decorative dolly, his shinobi shozoku glowing under the shining blacklights. Jiggling towers of yellow goo—"dessert"—slid across the tablecloth. The conversation dwindled, giving Jack a slim shot to deflect probing questions of strategy for the weekend's conference. He turned to Ezekiel with obvious intent.

"Have I told you about the MAGA Carta Masquerade? The budding movement?"

Amante swallowed the bait whole. "Hush up puta, mama explains better."

Her drunk was showing; four glasses of champagne in an hour could tranquilize a petite tiger. Amante scooted her chair close to Zeke and clamped a paw on his hemmed knee, stumbling through an attempted conversion ritual in the name of absolute monarchy. Ezekiel hailed from east-central Florida and could catch a whiff of bullshit from the gulf side.

"What separates your purge of egalitarian ideals from other *elitist* philosophies?"

Amante simmered in her seat; she loathed that e-slur, a cannonball decimating her upper deck but landing right where it belonged.

"Take our present surroundings, for example. You are enjoying yourself, far removed from the ruckus of the sidewalks below. A restoration of the throne marks a return to safety and beauty."

Jack almost concurred; after his brush with hell from the mugging and his glimpse of heaven through Penny, some semblance of law and order sounded alright.

"What about the late-period Romanov dynasty, the buffoon of a tsar fumbling so hard that even a zealot like Lenin had no trouble seizing power," Zeke said.

"Whataboutism is for those chimping out online once all other arguments run dry. It's basic physics. For every example, an equal and opposite counterexample. The reign of the Tudors."

This measuring of royal dicks unfolded until their water brought the "check"—a diamond-encrusted tablet for Amante to scan her fingerprint—and three tiny bathrobes.

"The food here is rare, delicious, but heavy on the neurotoxins. Sweating them out within a half-hour is highly recommended."

A session in the wood-lined sauna commenced without protest, Amante's heavily-doctored secondary sex characteristics practically bursting forth from the dam of her robe. Even Zeke wasn't that down bad with lust or loneliness; he invested an extra dose of sweat equity trying to fend off her advances, though she managed to grab a handful of his exposed junk a couple of times. Jack slipped away to source bleach for his retinas and explore this "semi-nude" spa, finding the toned bodies of wealthy matrons and their maître d's on full display beneath a skylight shaped like the moon. Through the steam, he glimpsed casual coitus taking the place of comradery in private rooms sporting translucent walls. With society regressing from organized Christianity, the upper crust seemed poised to repaganize, adopting a survival-of-the-fittest worldview in lieu of glorifying the weak. The consequences downstream remained to be seen.

The floor of the *Kongresszentrum* resembled an African bazaar, nations and corporations occupying vivid booths arranged like an open-air labyrinth, shilling grins greeting foot traffic in hopes of hawking a bulk order of double-neck bass guitars or finding international partners to pay the studio tab for horse-headed fiddlers. A banner hanging over the hall, a geopolitical sword of Damocles, announced that in light of the anniversary of that horrific war waged by a despot, the Eur-808 platinum sponsors had decided to include a "Spotlight on Ukraine" in this year's program, as both fundraiser for munitions and showcase for talent from the UK. Brochures distributed at the entrance carried an auxiliary announcement, proclaiming that the United Kingdom had relinquished its two-letter country code to the beleaguered Ukrainians, "in solidarity."

Amante sighed. "That stuffy word has gone the way of the buffalo, utilized every which way 'til mass extinction."

Thinking ahead, Jack informed her that, "Thinking ahead, I invited the delegation of label reps from Ukraine to your cabaret performance."

"I don't need to piggyback on those breadbasketcases for my *opera* to be successful."

Jack winced, but she bowed out of a follow-up haymaker.

"However, that may turn out to be a sharp tactic. I'll congratulate you if it works."

With her puta on a tight leash, Amante prowled the musical marketplace, allowing Jack to embarrass himself on her behalf each time she spotted an organization she wanted to invite to her Magna Carta jamboree that afternoon. She printed scrolls with date and time and capsule description, forcing Jack to hand them to potential patrons with the canned line, "we hope our opera makes you sing." The message was often lost in translation for reasons other than the perpetual language barrier. Whenever corporate ambassadors or tax-credit diplomats offered them a seat and a water-with-gas and an elevator's ride to explain further, Amante quickly left her element behind, struggling to articulate why the country of Azerbaijan should support an American song-and-dance that torched a British legal document from the Dark Ages.

"This will be a crucial talking point in the decades to come. It's like Apple in the '80s, as an opera."

Jack's formerly broad shoulders were crippled from durational cringing. Amante was no saleswoman, even for the topic she knew best, and the constant invocation of Wall Street stock pitches from her ex-husband's investing playbook only sunk them deeper in music industry quicksand. Jack boosted the morale, aware that his upcoming paychecks depended not on closing the best deal, but on warping Amante's perception of this old-world sojourn as money and man-hours well-spent.

"The stage we booked for the performance is in a compact room, and I invited over a hundred true-blue professionals via email. We shouldn't have trouble scoring a packed house."

Amante begrudgingly allowed him to work the floor solo, his standard style, more suitable here than their haphazard tag-team, a fiction declared with greater persuasion than an entire morning's worth of cabaret invitations. After the click-clack racket of Amante's two-grand high heels faded into the low rumble of the assembly, Jack quickly fled to the adjoining hotel. The lobby was filled with in-demand record producers and body-odored acquisitioneers. Ezekiel was hiding in the smoker's lounge, next to an upscale vending machine that sold cigarettes by the carton. The two men commiserated about the spa debacle.

"I see you made it out alive. Did Amante manage to deflower you?" Jack said.

"Your dear master thinks my ass is up for sale simply because she owns yours."

Amante's status as a potential financial asset forced Zeke to politely demur and head home alone instead of rejecting her loving touch outright, a feat of social acrobatics resulting in his present mode of avoidance.

"Fear not, I ditched her for the afternoon."

Frederic George, a renowned British talent manager with the power and experience to make or break stars, ducked into the lounge for a tobacco-laced breather, picking the plush-chair next to Ezekiel in order to roll up a fresh dart before offering them the bag of shag.

"The Queen's snout burns bright."

Jack accepted the clippings, constructing his own cigarette from gum-paper and looseleaf brown, a mostly European fad popularized in response to the skyrocketing price of a twenty-pack. The wave failed to reach New York, and he could see why, relighting his structurally-compromised cylinder after each puff. Zeke handed him a proper smoke.

Frederic chuckled. "Is this your first Eur-808?" Affirmative. "Bad hand to draw, it's a ghost town this year."

The two old dogs griped about the state of affairs in their mutual business, namely the way economically-viable distribution through physical media had been gutted by streaming platforms that taught consumers to devalue individual works of art.

"CDs used to cost around ten pounds. Now, the full history of mainstream music is available for the same price. Teach me how that math makes sense."

Zeke outlined the basic tenets of his plan to systematize a method of countercultural patronage, an ambitious design nevertheless delivered with erudition.

"Cheers to you if it works, and if it lasts. I'm fortunate to retain professional relationships from decades past. Helps with placement of new songs in and above the algorithms. Hopefully the thin thread left of the status quo lasts until my retirement."

An atmosphere of respect settled among the room's ashtrays, the pair of seasoned workhorses aware of their roles as generals on opposing sides of the battle for creative scraps.

Jack piped in. "I mingle with the occasional pop songstress in Manhattan. Maybe I could hook you up with a future chart-topper for a new client."

His roundabout approach to networking served its purpose, and an amused Frederic passed Jack a card printed with his direct line. An enthusiast of the grand tradition of British poetry, Ezekiel consummated the fresh acquaintanceship by reciting a few stanzas from *Goblin Market*, his silky tenor rendering the rhymes with reserved fanfare. Jack's hunch was again confirmed: there's no way this sensitive elder could have raped all those women.

Amante chose that moment to barge into their boy's club, waving a hand in front of her nose, making a fuss about the smoke in a smoker's lounge, her lips on the verge of forming the name PUTA before relaxing when she spotted Zeke. She stood in front of the three seated men like an auction-block broad, waiting to be greeted and introduced to the stranger. Frederic made a show of checking his silver timepiece before excusing himself to greener pastures. Alone with her dining companions, Amante batted her heavy lashes and addressed Ezekiel.

"Hello my *wittle* mouse, you left mommy kitten alone on the scary streets last night."

The baby voice was unflattering enough for someone half her age. Zeke made a show of kissing her prematurely liver-spotted hand and excusing himself for a catnap before the big "opera" performance commencing in a couple hours.

Amante scowled at Jack. "Who was that other gentleman? And why are we having a meeting in this tarpit?"

"He's a major player for the English-language labels. I told him about your work, but he didn't seem all that interested. And this wasn't a meeting until you rudely intruded."

Her spite was overwhelmed with concern that she had violated unspoken decorum, an aspirational aristocrat's fixation on etiquette in place of a ruler's sensibility.

"I have to dress myself in the vestments and brief the backup dancers. Be at the rented room a half hour beforehand to greet our guests by name."

Jack obeyed the keeper of the coffers, occupying his post by the sound-proofed door after wolfing down two döner wraps and a sack of peppered frites. To his surprise, as if the stated outcome had tapped into some current of chaos magic forming a crystalline web above the conference, a legion of global distributors and journalists filed into the small performance hall, curiosity piqued by this middle-aged woman's high-falutin' pedigree and her website's padded CV. The majority of the attendees came adorned with lapel pins, sporting the blue and yellow bars of the Ukrainian flag. It was difficult to determine who was a genuine nationalist; the sales of accoutrement, signalling support for the warhawk's cause, had tripled since the invasion, the same day that present moralists could, for the very first time, point to a map and correctly indicate the object of their heroic awareness campaigns.

The last straggler secured a seat, Jack closed the door, the fluorescents dimmed, the halogens flashed, and Amante goose-stepped towards center-stage, her Crumbian folds of Colombian flesh obscured by the cloak and jabot of a masculine judge's uniform, to perform a monologue, mocking the legal basis for common law through caricature. A man in the front row cackled, likely astounded into thinking the subject of derision was any number of human-rights violators and not the opposite, until his neighbor whispered in his direction. Tinny scratch-tracks played from a boombox, disguised as a tree stump. Six men in drab tunics and breeches can-canned from behind a curtain, their muffled voices singing a word-salad medley praising the generosity of god-like kings. Amante stripped off her robes with dramatic flourish, revealing royal garments reimagined for burlesque, the breakaway velcro syncing with the peasants' falling to their knees, one lucky actor permitted to fondle the hem of her magenta skirt. Jack waited for her scepter to be used for raunchy pole antics, an angle only implied. The lyrics of her tone-deaf tune were pining for ascendance to the throne amid a bloodless coup. She resorted to base crowd-work, encouraging the industry professionals, in attendance to assess the tricks and merits of falsely-advertised opera, to stand up and clap along to the pan flute obbligato. Near the conclusion of six minutes that felt closer to six-hundred and sixty-six, Amante climbed on the sturdy spines of her troupe, a Middle Ages cheerleader's pyramid, and reached for the sickeningly high final note, holding it through the strength of lungs weaned on domestic screaming matches and clearing a third of the audience in the process. Thrilled by her historically-revisionist diet-striptease, the Ukrainian delegation applauded vigorously, a ritual that shifted into staccato hand claps on the downbeat, in unison, a testament to their collectivist agrarian roots.

"What did they write?"

"I'm not trained to interpret the acrylic alphabet."

"It's *cyrillic*. Translate the article."

"I don't have a smartphone."

"Use mine for fuck's sake, I'm too nervous to read it."

"Ok, ok, the title seems to be ARF."

"ARF?"

"It's an acronym. 'Ancien Régime Farce.'"

Eur-808 had grown more streamlined the longer it reigned, a favor to the busymen. Seven days of activity burdened the official calendar, but all serious business took place on the first. The media machine earned its overtime, dashing out reviews of the afternoon's showcases during a full-coffee-pot night. Pleased with the applause in the room, Amante was treating Jack to brunch in her suite. Risking these good tidings on red, Jack read aloud the cultural write-up, given prime position on the homepage of eastern arts newspaper *The Lviv Hammer*.

"Colombian-American composer-activist Amante wowed a packed house yesterday with the premiere of her humorous cabaret. There was singing (bad on purpose), dancing (used to hilarious effect) and live theater (deeply parodied), all in service of a single theme: the global rise of fascist leaders who imagine themselves as sovereign kings on the ruins of democratic castles. Amante wittily mocks this disgusting tendency in six action-packed minutes of performance from the right side of history. Even the title 'opera' is a winking joke for savvy viewers—"

The rattling of a porcelain cup in the cold fury of her grip disturbed his recap.

"Look, maybe this fool missed the point, but it's a small regional outlet, plus the best way to attract converts is if unsuspecting youth believe your cause is actually dedicated to the contrary, you know?"

Amante stirred her latte with a shellac fingernail, relishing a moment of contemplation.

"Perhaps you're correct, puta. If this piece leads to distribution opportunities in some shithole of a country, the opera's messaging could very well become subliminal."

Jack harbored doubts but allowed his mercurial boss to fly back to New York on a positive note. Again the captain of his own clock, he conscripted Ezekiel, né Rip Van, for a lark around Berlin. They explored the ex-Soviet side of the crumbled Wall, marking three-letter initials in white ink. A billboard for a luxury watch manufacturer, infected with the graffiti parasite, simply stated GENOCIDE. An astrologer's secret staircase in a hollow tower stood tall above an international mall chain. Not in the market for perfume or cardboard pizza or bidets or duvets or DVD boxsets by Duvernay, the boys decided to whittle away the daylight hours at a nearby gallery.

In truly German fashion, the austere white-walled space hosted but a single work, a bulwark against the rampant overstimulation to be found in classical museums, the head typically spinning with portraits and landscapes and still-lifes after only an hour. At the far end of the minimalist establishment was a massive mirror, the words I AM NORMAL GUY spray-painted in neon green across the surface. Dozens of visitors posed for photos in the reflection, a few attempting limitless autocopies by flipping the camera around, cropping out the colorful verbiage entirely. Dozens more held their phones to their heads as if on a call.

"Who could all these people possibly be talking to?" Jack whispered to Ezekiel, quickly realizing that the black bricks were audio tour-guide devices.

A placard explaining the piece concluded with the phrase, "*Danke Schön,* Snapchat!"

Ezekiel reviewed the experience upon exiting: "Art sucks."

The duo wound their way to a Eur-808 afterparty at the Canadian embassy. Frozen gel cubes of maple syrup were served as dessert by paid-for babes in head-to-toe denim. Thumping bass hits echoed from a steep staircase hidden inside the staff library, and a careful descent past writhing bodies revealed a hockey rink converted into a dance-floor for the evening. Zeke bobbed and weaved around thrashers and shufflers to find the bar. Jack chatted with a man in designer overalls: a music producer, as expected; one based in New York, less expected; who had skimmed and enjoyed the article about Amante's cabaret act, entirely unexpected.

"If you liked that, you'll love this."

Jack proceeded to spin a narrative about Penny Delphine, a homeless girl with a voice like a cherubic choir who was in talks with an ace manager and already had a killer promoter. She was a gorgeous, far-from-shy starlet who just needed a little professional help in the studio. Fenix Williams, the producer, agreed to meet her once he returned to Manhattan, and Jack grabbed his card.

Zeke returned with three gin-and-tonics and a Romanian witch, her hair a thick shock of dark curls. She fed them a tab of acid apiece and led them to the pit where the music was loudest. The newly-minted trio cut a rug while the synthetic psychedelics kicked in. Jagged motion turned fluid and the isolated dancers morphed into one mass: an archetypal hyperrhythm. The chemical fairy melted away into the black. Jack and Zeke tripped to the corner to take a break for conversation.

"She could be a real drag, but at my age any attention from a young filly is something to cherish. This may have been the last time."

Jack forgot the name or attitude of the chick on his arm in New York and stuck to generalized advice.

"There's plenty of fish in the sea, even at the age of sixty-three."

Ezekiel laughed, sexual concerns disintegrated by the subwoofers. The two of them trekked home in the rain before braving the metro, a rising sun revealing the stark difference between spacey, giggling Americans and the stern Germans riding the rails to Monday morning jobs of sweat and toil. Deep-fried beyond belief, Zeke conked out on the couch while Jack opted for a surreal session in his inbox. Up first was another note from Penny.

Precious Jack, please clear your calendar the first weekend upon returning. It's our birthday, and I'm throwing us a party. With love, PD.

Another selfie with one of his Jack-stickers, this one stuck to a vanilla ice cream cone, mid-lick. His sweet reverie dissolved with the next email, the latest in a long one-sided thread from the weirdest of his old friends. On a scroll through the months, he spotted an assortment of pictures of himself, with comments like *JUST FOUND THIS PIC OF YOU. HAHA. GOOD TIMES.* Some messages contained only his name and a question mark. Jack glanced at the newest communiqué to ignore.

IS THIS YOU? I KNOW YOU'RE NOT ONLINE.

Two blue hyperlinks. He clicked the first, a *Post* article about the MAGA Carta Masquerade. Finally! The writer was somewhat dismissive of the affair, the dreaded phrase "turgid elitism" making an appearance midway down the page; he also acknowledged his willingness to attend a fabulous party, no matter how revolting the raison d'etre. The header image was a wide shot of keynote speaker Gabriel Rosemont, with Jack in the foreground. The caption identified Big G, but not Young J. No Amante name-drops in sight, amusing Jack to no end. He clicked the second link, a thread from a salty "digital author" complaining about the event, projecting race politics onto a zoomed-in photo of Jack.

Look at his smirk. This is the ideal specimen to front their Great White Regime.

Below were thousands of replies and quote tweets.

Disgusting nazis.

Fuk white supremacy.

More like look at his jawline.

TFW you don't mispronounce your order at the taco truck.

TND 4 life.

DAE think he's hot?

Where is this?

Magna Chad!

Me when I get away with minor theft at the supermarket.

This is the face of the past, not the future.

Supreme Leader Magna Chad.

3
U.W.S.

"My coming to New York had been a mistake; for whereas I had looked for poignant wonder and inspiration in the teeming labyrinth. . . I had found instead only a sense of horror and oppression which threatened to master, paralyze, and annihilate me."

— H.P. Lovecraft

The last remaining artist squat in lower Manhattan held fast to an ironic station, positioned a few blocks from the steel-girder obelisk christening a live-work-play-die district for inbound yuppies, strip mall as friendly neighborhood, where the police force is privatized and the sculptural vortex serves as a portal to hell only for those who jump. Despite its role for the past year as a hip living room venue—hosting first-draft autofiction singalongs and theater edging from behind the fourth wall, "actors" that "play" horny "characters" then try to blow out the backs of innocent viewers—the management never managed to hang a sign, informing the uninitiated that the industrial vault door did in fact lead to a creative carnival of dissidents, revolutionaries, and apocalyptic sects, and not some Son of Sam meets H.H. Holmes copycat killhouse.

Upon entering, and not for his virgin rodeo, Jack remembered why there was such need for discretion. A sentient cloud of cigarette smoke practically threw out the welcome mat. A lanky broad with pixie cut and push-up bra poured liquor sans license behind the makeshift bar. The place was an inferno in-training, volumes of Dante and German philosophy and Italian pop-culture and epistolary novellas stacked at twice his height around the room's baseboards. If the New York City fire department, with funky per-squad nicknames like sports franchises, The Fighting Dragons and The Permanent Wildcats and The Welcoming Chinamen—if the heroes of 9/11 didn't shut down the festivities, a bookworm's avalanche certainly would.

Apparently the "owner" maintained an apartment upstairs, a place for e-girls to recline and snort lines in his bed without crossing the line by giving him head. He shuffled around the premises during events and performances, allegedly born in the late '70s in Brooklyn but bearing a beard and posture that screamed "I established the Bolsheviks in the Kremlin."

The furthest reaches of the shotgun squat opened up into high ceilings stapled with the cross-stitched skins of vintage couches. There was a staircase going nowhere fast on steps of dark brown wood, and during crowded evenings the top was the best seat a general-admissioner could swipe; Jack called it the captain's chair. That night, the space filled only to half-capacity, but every face that wished him well was vaguely recognized, greetings with grins and fist bumps and exclamations of "Magna Chad in da building!" A homebrewed banner hung above the partition between extended foyer and performance hall, halfway decent calligraphy reading MAGNA CHAD COMES TO TOWN.

In a skirmish against over-stimulation, Jack found solace with social butterfly Penny Delphine, who stood glowing near the green corner in an ankle-length dress of flattering proportions. The fabric was printed with juicy red cherries, a perfect match for his patchwork tablecloth fruit-shirt. She greeted him with a brief peck on the lips and a tight hug, fairly conservative for a reunion after four weeks apart. The hour was early and her cup was mostly full.

"Do you dig the theme?"

Most attendees were decked out in chic-tacky 'fits of clashing colors. Jack pondered his answer to the riddle.

"I told everyone to dress like your meme."

His final two weeks in Europe had failed to stop the spread, an organic peer-to-peer contagion of Magna Chad jokes and reaction GIFs. With his face plastered over every handheld screen in the scene and no social profiles to mitigate or control the data flow, Jack's anonymity was preserved in name alone; a legion of tweeters could pick him out of a line-up but few could find his file in a folder.

"Happy birthday." Penny eyed him—with a glint of seduction?—and promised he'd get his gift later.

"Happy birthday to you too. Thanks for setting this in motion."

The daisychain of lamps flickered thrice. She squeezed his hand. "You arrived right in time for the show."

Jack picked a spot near the "stage": an open zone of concrete floor. The other guests filed in, chattering like cold teeth. A twelve-year-old picked at an acoustic guitar, warming up his prepubescent fingers while Penny fiddled with a corded microphone.

"I'll need lots of reverb, crank it please."

A few audiophiles laughed. Some geek crawled to her amp to make the adjustment. Jack mouthed a silent hello to Gwen, who pulled up a chair next to him, her phone camera pointing in the direction of his forthcoming reaction. The overhead lights dimmed, a projector beamed the same chiseled photo of Magna Chad, and Penny slowly slid into a sultry crouch, bellowing the gorgeous opening note of a power ballad, accompanied by the young boy's shimmering slide guitar. The song's mournful tone, complete with forlorn lyrics about craving the attention of a faraway lover, gave way to an upbeat disco section, Penny writhing and singing about how Jack hacked her algorithm. He blushed, the darkness hiding his rosy coloration from Gwen's "Jack Valentine Reacts To Biographical Track" video.

Trotsky of Tribeca opened wide his crusty gaze for the first time in a half-century, rushing to turn down the volume and yellin' about how Penny was "GONNA GET MY OLD ASS EVICTED!" She compensated with an ever-more extravagant ballyhoo, her facial expressions reflecting the humor and tragedy of the song. Rock and fucking roll. After a show-stopping finale, some folks clapped but otherwise returned to their boring conversations and shitty wine. Jack embraced Penny; Gwen continued to film, before finding her wits and her misplaced social cue to cease fire. Penny had acted fast, tying herself to his side in the social eye, a coronation, the merging of their respective kingdoms in a shared universe of related nonsense.

"That was terrific," he told her. "What were those last lyrics?"

"I know your retard brain can't fathom words set to music. I was singing 'Repopulate the nation.'"

Jack digested her long-term proposal. Eavesdropped reviews came flooding in.

"That was so erratic."

"You mean erotic? She's super sexy."

The alcohol poured freely, copious and liberal amounts of backstock from the raided cellars of previous, paying tenants, liters to intoxicate woodland militias repurposed for a handful of enthusiasts drunk under the sign of Arte.

"Who was that kid in your band?"

"I found him busking in Tompkins Square and recruited him for the PD cause. My initials also stand for Police Department. It's another dog-whistle."

He spoke into her unruly mop of natural blonde hair. "Glad I scooped you up fresh off the boat. The men in this scene are either simps or wolves."

She tugged at his shirt, wanting to crawl inside. "What does that make you?"

"I'll show you when we get back to my apartment."

She grabbed his hand and forced it against her ample chest. He squeezed, relishing the first chance to assess what she was packing.

"My body will be yours after we're married."

He didn't believe her, thinking the commitment to the bit would crumble, that the walls of continence would fall, all in due course after a little more intense courtship. Jack had whored himself out to all flavors of women over the years; mostly reformed, he settled on only pursuing sex within the bounds of a serious relationship.

The city's quietest aux-cord DJ pressed play, and the partygoers took a brief tour of duty as stagehands to clear the floor of furniture and clutter. Penny pulled Jack out of their private kissing booth and back into the center of attention to dance.

"I collected thirteen hours of songs into a playlist for this event, no one ever relinquishes control even though I have the best taste here, it's a shame really," she said, easily heard over pianissimo breakbeats.

Not a single additional soul flocked to the twist 'n' shout town square, so the most popular couple in the room maximized their use of space to experiment with unrehearsed aerial work, Penny's legs wrapped around Jack's torso, her dress hiked up without revealing much, the pair swaying back and forth to mumble rap better suited for soda commercials. Another Midwest transplant, an oldhead friend of Penny's who allegedly lost his right forearm "in the Cold War"—this guy picked a fistfight with the squat's czar after the ex-Chekist tried to shake his hand, poorly timed with a wry utterance of *"spasibo,"* so Jack and his four-date fiance busted a French exit uptown to his latest sublet, a two-bedroom two blocks off the west lip of Central Park. His new roommate was still calcified on the massive couch, shredding on a plastic axe while multi-colored notes flew out from the TV screen towards the player.

"Is this game an homage to that iconic train film from the Lumineers?" Jack asked of an unresponsive Timothy, noise-cancelling cans operating at full-blast. Jack filled a glass with tap water and joined Penny in yet another other-person's chamber of rest.

"Thank you, I'm terribly dehydrated." She grabbed for the glass, taking a small sip.

"Do you want to borrow a shirt to sleep in?"

Jack made a show of averting his gaze. She changed into a tiny white tee, revealing her statuesque physique through a screen-printed graphic reading "I ♡ PR." She giggled—"it's a little tight"—and went in for another sip of water, purposefully missing her mouth and dumping the contents across her chest.

"Oh my, look what I've done!"

"Let's get you out of that before you catch a cold," Jack said, stripping off her top and hanging it up to dry.

She glanced down. "I've never shown them to a boy before."

There was a pause, potent with lust, then Jack pounced on his willing prey, kissing and licking and fondling. They edged each other senseless with hours of heavy petting before falling asleep, forehead to forehead.

Bar billiards abided by strict guidelines of succession, a right-to-left line of keys, quarters, or driver's licenses to indicate who can rack next. A deep-downtown watering hole filled with minor irritations—gauche Halloween decor, obnoxious bartenders feigning deaf ignorance, patrons with extra chromosomes—bucked the trend, renting out resin balls for fifteen bucks an hour. Jack once logged so many shifts alone at the table that management invited him to stay after closing time, smoke cigarettes indoors, and drink for free. This round found him squaring off against one Simone Richards: shady financier, potential ally, kinda hot. Jack lined up for the break. The bird-like woman elaborated on her visions.

"There's a strong undercurrent of bohemian, right-leaning energy scattered across lower Manhattan. I want to capture it."

Default progressivism had unearthed the fault lines in the American regime over the past eight years, with the neutered quakes of conservatism barely registering on the Richter scale; real power assembled elsewhere, bloodless corporate overlords at the top and antifa foot-soldiers at the bottom, a geological pincer movement to astroturf topsy-turvy values upon the formerly green grass of Capitol Hill.

Seven stripes, seven solids, a black and a white scattered across the cheetah-print felt; no sinkers.

"My games always start this way," Jack said.

Simone took her turn to miss. "Moral duels are fought with cultural pistols, why else would the FBI and the CIA—"

"Yeah yeah, even the Coast Guard keeps an office of script doctors in Hollywood." Jack crushed a bank shot.

"Exactly, it's all downstream from entertainment." Another swing and a miss for Simone. "Take your girlfriend's show the other night."

Jack hadn't seen the Svengali doll in attendance, and the reference carried a hint of menace.

"The dog-whistles were to die for, and most of the smooth-brains watching had no clue. They were simply enjoying the music, letting the secret messages sink into their unconscious, silky-smooth minds."

Jack maintained his neutral 8-ball expression and sank another two.

"But that *russkii* crackhead running the place couldn't manage a book club, much less an event with any number of moving parts. Sound, image, staff, refreshments, the list goes on as the guests increase."

Simone almost made a long-distance shot, clearing the path for Jack to score once more.

"I'm about to put a down payment on this penthouse downtown, and I aim to transform it into a functional venue. Art and politics, but not in a cringe leftie way. Concerts, readings, screenings, debates. Opportunities abound."

Jack nailed a three-hit streak, striking out on the black, exasperated with this sidewinding offer.

"Hey lady, I dig the ambition, but what's this got to do with me? You want press or something?"

"That might ruin the mystique of an exclusive club before we even begin. All journalists are bastards. AJAB."

Simone smirked and sank a full set of eight, in a row. Better a hustler than a hooker. Glad he for once didn't let his big mouth bet on his pool chops, Jack tuned in close to the anchor of her pitch.

"I want your help. Show up, make the place cool, invite good-looking gals. Bring me business, if you can."

Jack re-racked the balls for a rematch, a hopeless quest for petty revenge.

"Your turn to break."

Simone planted a soft, feminine hand in the air between them, an act of typical good-game camaraderie reduced here to a devil's bargain: Jack's apolitical posturing traded for niche infamy in the new counterculture, plus twenty percent of gross profits. The hippies were right-wing! Jack smelled a fed, pseudonymous purse strings attached to tin-cans between the heat of the street and some SuperPAC. Perhaps Simone was one of the good ones, a friend near the highest place once the reigns of control inevitably switched back to the true winners—or a rich ticket to the bunker if everything went south.

They shook hands. "Besides, I saw that flurry of memes. Magna Chad. Good brand. You're the poster boy of the movement now."

On his way home, Jack swung through a supermarket, loading his basket with the typical items, yellow onions, lean chicken breast and an assortment of ingredients for once-daily super-smoothies: bananas and blueberries, coconut shavings and flax seed, walnuts and Greek yogurt, almond butter and steel-cut oats. He grabbed a jug of milk, sourced from somewhere other than the cow's udder, a holdover from a past era spent tailing the hoi polloi into veganism.

Grocery acquisition was the stubbed toe of select New Yorkers, many opting to exclusively dine out, order online, or take seven small trips per week to purchase rations for the following twenty-four hours. Jack didn't mind the eighteen-block walk with a full paper bag cradled in each arm, enjoying the simple act of planning ahead, a single regimen amid an unstable life of lawlessness.

The fifth-floor hike-up reeked of bodega joints. His absent roommate must have hotboxed the living room then fled the scene by fire-escape. Jack's sundown solitude barely allowed for a clogged exhale and a goose-honk coughing fit before his flip rang, an inbound call from Penny Delphine.

"I was just thinking of you." True or not, he had indeed been craving another appointment with her warm body after the other night's unfinished session.

"You haven't snuck out of my mind since the moment we met."

She caught him up on what he had missed at the six o'clock Mass. His father, a kitchen-sink comedian, had a stock routine about Catholics: sit down, stand up, kneel, repeat. The punchline was something about aerobic exercise for the kingdom of God.

"The homily was beautiful, a righteous damnation of the impurities of disordered love. There's a proper way to do these things, you know."

Her poetic opinions resembled icebergs; he sensed much left unsaid.

"We probably shouldn't make a habit of the other night," she continued.

Jack clenched his jaw, afraid to lose access to a woman he had only barely begun to know, in the biblical sense.

"Which part of the other night is troubling you, the fun or the affection?"

His responses in periods of emotional turmoil were optical illusions: some saw a lady, others a skull, some heard a dash of humor to cut the tension, others a verbal backhand.

"Cohabitation is the snowy crest of a slippery alpine slope, one that drops off into the second circle."

He pulled the phone away from his ear for a few heartbeats, fully rattled. He figured the pursuit of pleasure with an adult convert would be a bloody uphill battle, his pleas and appeasements chewed up by St. Michael's machine gun, but the thought of sleeping next to one another as a theater of misplaced moralizing was beyond the pale.

"I believe that men and women in committed relationships should at least lay beside each other, it's a sweet act of intimacy," he said, hoping she couldn't detect the elevated feelings in his voice.

"That's not my belief system."

"Why don't you settle for a milquetoast bible-study tubthumper then?" he grumbled, the false sense of a personal slight creating the urgent need to defend, to escalate into conflict.

"Because I want you, your good heart, your strong constitution. But it won't be easy, I understand that."

She went on to explain the half-year enrollment in Catholic marriage prep classes, a requirement for the blessing of a distant deity, one that would surely end with him bending the knee and promising to raise their children under the tortured awning of the faith, drafting a new brood of Jesus-freaks to refresh the ranks of the Church.

"I'd prefer to expose kids to a wide range of ideas." There was a pause. "And teach them to farm the land, care for animals, train with handguns."

Penny laughed, the sweetest sound's second coming. "I'm glad we're on the same page about a couple things." There was a longer pause. "Why are we future-tripping so hard right now?"

It was a turn-of-phrase Jack's mother employed during social work when her clients fixated on the longview, gray areas beyond their domain to affect.

"You're right, we're still honeymooners, let's have some fun."

He felt her grow somber at the far end of the line.

"I'm not here to have fun. You fret over these bodily concerns. I'm worried about our eternal souls. To live like pagans, cuddling and fornicating out of wedlock, makes us no better than all the unrepentant sodomites raving in the bowels of this city. I'm *in* this world, but not *of* this world. Too many mortal and venial sins produce attachments, weighing us down when it's time to stand trial at the gates of Heaven. I want to be with you forever, in paradise."

During his fedora'd stint on r/atheism, the natural swing of the pendulum after a strict Methodist rearing, Jack would have shrugged off this psychospiritual babble as sheer lunacy, the product of an unhinged mind clinging to a worldview deemed appropriate but dated by modern civilization. But the humanist NGO organizing principles of inclusion and diversity were the sand upon which the crumbling castle stood. His recent fascination was the lost Arte of shaping reality, a practice washed away by the creeping technoparadigm of corporate hypersigils and a horizon too dense with signs to see, much less to think. New-age magicians were drowned not by stones tied to feet, but by a permanent deluge of information. The invisible kings knew the tricks of Solomon's trade, hiding machine demons between the circuits, living code brainwashing the innocent into slurping up insect slop and taking pride in their toe tags. Amid widespread decay, a tilt towards the esoteric seemed sane. Penny's passion for traditional Catholicism was a twin flame, a different route to comparable conclusions. Christians burning witches was so passé; in this latter day, they could be bedfellows aligned against a rotting center.

Penny and Jack continued their marathon three-hour phone call until her willpower collapsed, and he paid for a taxi to ferry her across the river.

"My desire to see you outweighs my qualms, for now." An ominous qualifier. "And this time you had a turban-clad accomplice to whisk me away against my will. Warrant me dual citizenship in Stockholm."

In lieu of a sizzling comeback, Jack's lungs were seized by another doubled-over flurry of coughs, viral or spiritual. Penny responded in-kind, hacking aggressively into her palms, infected or empathetic.

"The doctors have given me one month to live," each said, in their own words, practically in unison, giggling in spite of the rote material.

Jack slapped a staccato drum beat down his chest. "If I pass, don't let them harvest these organs. My driver's license stands as evidence of my dying wish."

"I don't even have a driver's license, but my guts must remain in this body until the resurrection."

Jack made a game of trying to identify each internal part by poking around her belly, an exercise fast devolving into tickle terror. "I won't let anyone hurt you or your insides, passenger princess."

Penny howled. "Who's going to protect me from you?"

Further explorations of the Upper West Side on-foot revealed a wealth of bizarre details. On the corner of Athletics and Misguided, a rolling banner ad promoted an upcoming tournament for blind, paraplegic fencers.

"At least they can't poke each other's eyes out."

"Can I buy them bus tickets instead?"

Near the intersection of Gastronomy and Humiliation: a militant pizza parlor, where conscripts who bake poor pies must stand on a pedestal of shame and silently give complimentary slices to pedestrians.

"Freedom isn't free..."

"If you can read this, thank a teacher. If it's not in Italian, thank a veteran."

With a background in floral design, Penny soon secured her first NYC job at a ritzy florist for decrepit Upper East yentas. She skipped through Central Park to rejoin Jack, fresh arrangements in tow, and recounted her first shift at the flower shop, a seven-hour block of manual labor in high heels. She had bumped into plants, knocked over vases, and spilled jars of cuttings, celestial slapstick, a seraph adjusting to the form of flesh. She was fussed at by slavedriver bosses who could condemn a girl for her very essence then invite her to dinner with sleazy intent.

"Yoko was right, women are the niggers of the world. Even poor Leda, defiled by a false and craven god."

"She seems to enjoy that swan's sniffer in her snatch, at least in the paintings I've seen."

Fresh grass on Olmstead's hills invited frolicking leisure in the spring, a time for lovers, and couples sprouted everywhere they turned, on benches and rocks and paved paths, perhaps some even getting frisky under woodland canopies. Many seemed like ill-advised pairings, latent quarantine connections, two individuals sitting together, scrolling in mixed company. Jack and Penny schemed about plans for the rest of the day.

"Do you want to go to Mass with me?"

"Didn't you go yesterday?"

"I attended every day, back home."

"Was that sustainable?"

"Balanced with tap lessons and two jobs and various boyfriends and a reading group."

Jack simmered: she had been with other men since converting?

"That makes sense, I had an ex with a mucho cluttered calendar. She was studying French literature, then punched cards at a highbrow gentlemen's club where the girls only had to sway topless, plus she had a golden doodle diva of a dog that would yank off the covers and demand a morning walk. Homemaking was badly neglected, so much so that she once found cockroaches writhing in her unclean coffee maker."

Jack failed to mention that he had been fucking the girl's barred-out roommate for years before fucking her, or those hysterical night terrors at the prospect of abandonment, or the threesome with the prostitute who thought she was a boy, or the time they fucked when she came over crying after being raped by her drug dealer. The guy later got whacked by two hoodrats who sang R&B on the side. She had only been upset at other people for being upset.

"Our first date was spent watching that film with the typewriters and the bugs and the wives getting shot in the head instead of apples. That reminds me, instead of our nineteenth retarded scene party that advertises names of popular guests rather than proper entertainment, would you like to see a movie tonight?"

Penny stared past him, her sense of grounding all out of whack. "I'm not sure who's more autistic, you or I…"

Jack detected the disruption and, like a simpleton, attributed it to the wrong cause.

"I'd be happy to join you at Mass another time, but I have a business meeting at a fabulous hotel near the triangle beneath Canal St. There's a screen in the basement and the tickets have been purchased. Please join me there after you get done with church."

She smiled. "Now that's what every girl likes to hear."

Jack settled into the sunken cushions of the lounge, surrounded by a pool table, a jazz band and all manner of bars, for booze, oysters and cappuccinos. The ceiling towered far above him, impossible to dust, a work of architectural deception: openly-visible rooms abounded while the recesses of the hotel hid other wonders, disco-clubs and cinémathèques, fancy bathrooms to snort powder or shoot smack. He had it on good authority that the guy who had made all those sublime, dirty heroin movies in the '90s, about kings and lieutenants and hackers and vampires and Madonna, stayed there whenever he blew into town from Rome for a retrospective; but the couple of tweedledees sitting eagerly before Jack that evening were no able ferraris. Wham and Bam, birth names long forgotten or willfully hidden, were the fraternal scions of a legacy box car racer hailing from Navajo country, his children avoiding the speedometer's curse by building a scrappy start-up with no forebears, perhaps for good reason. Their media company, both an archive for collegiate researchers and a streamer for at-home enthusiasts, would be dedicated solely to performance art, a unanimously in-person pastime. Bam, the big brother, was interested in hiring Jack to promote the launch of the website through guerilla marketing tactics.

"What's the timeline?"

"Well...," began Wham, who did all the talking while Bam handled the emails, "our road map is a nod to Magellan, in that despite the missing sections and geographic inaccuracies, we're plotting a course to the finish line."

Their father would be so proud to learn of this pursuit of the checkered flag.

"There's chickens, then there's eggs, you know? Hard to gather clips of indigenous haircuts and cornbread crucifixions for environmental conservation without a hosting platform, hard to code the platform without the money, hard to source the cash without subscription revenue. We're thinking about tackling these tasks in reverse order and throwing a party to premier the site, which at first will just collect email addresses to hoard for future announcements."

Jack could commission helicopters to drop thousands of flyers, littering every square block from Yonkers to Staten, and these play-pretend business buffoons would still be staring at an empty sign-up sheet.

"What's your budget?"

At the first whiff of labor pro-bono, Jack took his leave to scurry downstairs, citing a picture-show date with a real looker, which impressed his non-clients to no end. Jack found his Penny lying supine on a floating Chesterfield, a maritime snack precluding the need for popcorn.

"Two, under Valentine."

The cashier printed, the attendant tore, and they settled into the front row like they owned the place, stowing armrests to sprawl among four assigned seats, her legs folded across his. During the opening reel, some inbred crept down to snap a phone picture of the screen as if it were a painting in an art gallery. Don't these mouthbreathers know that high-resolution scans are available online? But they want *their* sentimental attachment to *their* shitty photo, why bother looking at anything, simply bear witness through a six-inch rectangle of mediated experience like Koreans in the Vatican, in fact why spend hard-earned Democratic People's Republic *won* on airfare and lodging, surely an intrepid videographer or 3D-renderer had already mapped the interior in 1080p for YouTube.

After his rage expired, Jack found the film to be quite charming, an unorthodox courtship between two quirksters, he with his bushy moustache and she with her oversized indoor sunglasses, both offering talkative performances of heightened, hysterical realism, threats of suicide giving way to facial-hair shavings giving way to abject adoration. The leading lady had been married to the picture's maker.

"Directors do their best work with their wives. This John, and Jean-Luc…"

"Ingmar and Federico too. Shoot 'em like you love 'em."

Once the scroll of credits unfurled, they twirled each other on sidewalks under the light of the moon then shuttled one hundred blocks uptown on the A. Every train ride across the island was an amorous opportunity, her sitting on his lap or laying her weary head on his shoulder. They developed an unspoken agreement: in the public madhouse of the late-night transit system, Penny could sleep on Jack while he kept watch for slick thieves and schizophrenic beggars; in the private teleportation chamber of a taxi after dark, Jack could sleep on Penny while she gazed at skyscrapers.

"I've wanted to move here since I was thirteen," she said, shrugging off her coat and climbing into bed.

With the verbal summoning of that number, lucky or un-, cosmic or trite, the porous barrier between adolescence and womanhood, a few maroon spots appeared on the top-sheet below.

"Uh oh." Her cheeks grew a fainter shade of red.

"It's a relief to meet a girl who remembers how to blush."

She washed the blood from her legs and promised to launder his linens.

"I never learned how to handle this, every time is like the first. Blessed are the retards and their explosive menstruation."

"It's a testament to your feral roots."

"If you found me in a swamp, what would you do?"

"Establish a line of communication through clicks and whistles, then bring you back to my barn for domestication, leaving a touch of the wilderness intact for amusement and profit."

"We could cook up a sideshow act and take it on the road. I can even tap dance."

They tiptoed along the cobblestone path from playful riff to passionate kiss, then another, now a third, and then

116

she was chewing on his bicep and leaving deep indentations of bite marks across his muscular back, a fleeting cure for a consumptive spirit.

She came up for air, grinning. "I swear I'm not a succubus."

Jack's friend once warned him against such sex-crazed creatures after his fling charming a chick from her cubicle. The girlboss had begged Jack to slap her clean across the face at his neighborhood dive on the first date, then gifted him a toothbrush for her place on the second. By the third, she was encouraging him to join her on the family's island off the Panhandle.

With Penny stripped bare to her bra and his boxers, Jack spotted the dark squiggles of tattoo ink spilling out from her lower back.

"What's this...?" He shifted positions to investigate, finding a rough tramp stamp, rune-like pictograms arranged in columns of *tategaki*.

"I made them up while trapped at home with my ex and a cheap tattoo gun."

"He branded you." Jack pictured the infernal artist using his masterwork as target practice for backshots.

"Don't worry about all that. The past is nothing more than a shared hallucination." She flipped over to salvage the situation with a glum smooch, her best attempt to distract, the handbook of a child psychologist. "Your face is so gorgeous, a geological and genealogical feat."

He warmed back up and gripped her sides, hiding the cursèd black marks. "If my face were a rocky mountain, I'd provide you the supplies to climb."

"Gwen showed me a tweet about your jawline. It's a blessing to caress your most popular feature."

The memeification of Jack Valentine brought a score of additional introductions, most as unapologetically foul as the Wham-Bam knockoff AbramoFlix jam from the other night: audio diary chronicling mass cancellation, non-profit fighting reverse racism of artificial intelligence, verité docuseries about fictionalized motivational speaker, country album recorded in condemned mine as commentary on deindustrialization of Rust Belt, and so many, *so many* social accounts in need of a boost, pages dedicated to pharmaceutical satire and teacher's assistant's union organizers watchdog groups, impersonations of fruit from the libertarian perspective and crossword puzzle awareness. Everyone had a pet project, each more stupid and convoluted than the last, all of them desperate for prefabricated clout. His was the chiseled face of the movement to repeal the Magna Carta for good, and the people flocked to his office hours to pay tribute and request a bequeathment of funds, thinking he had yanked that lavish masquerade from the depths of his own wallet. Jack was happy to accept the comped drinks and "I'll pick up the tab this first time" dinners, promising nothing in return. His position as gossip rag kingmaker had earned the ire of Amante, who had reduced the flow of capital until her cause was advanced.

"I think you should finance the scene. I've fielded dozens of pitches since we returned from Berlin, most of them quite asinine, yes, but all willing to acknowledge their patronage and shill your work to restore absolute monarchy, absolutely."

Amante stared daggers from across the refectory table. "And I'm sure this great goblet of cash will include a higher rate for you at the stem as project manager?"

Hell no, these were herds of ideas impossible to shepherd, she had his manipulations all twisted, was he an inferior student of Machiavelli?

"I'd rather you just reward me for quality consultation, but I won't turn down a higher rate if my services exceed their worth on paper."

"I've already fucked half the little boys of this scene, I don't want to leave money on their dressers too."

Jack implored her to reconsider; his recent experience as viral object had taught him the sticky power of a name, of a meme as a name and a name as a meme, QWERTY keyboards thundering with the repeated obsecration of magic keywords and the entire sphere of digital discourse could be rigged, should be reverse-engineered, would be won, the day was won Amante! Don't you understand!

"I propose spreading around your blank checks while you simultaneously seed a legend, *Amantellamonies*, it rolls right off the tongue. Our efforts are a stable of stalking horses and we can only take credit for the winners. You are the monarch, dispensing favorable judgements upon your loyal subjects. Lore wins!"

But flattery didn't; Amante brushed off his imaginative ranting as hysteria induced by a double espresso. She explained instead her plan for a book launch, an essay collection featuring the echolocation of prominent academics who justified her war against the Magna Carta—a concept entirely lacking in cachet, cool and hip left for dead in a ditch, side by side with two in each head. He couldn't promote such a lame view anymore or risk losing his budding influence, but he could reign from behind the safety of strings. No one suspected a holy fool, and prosocial matchmaking might solve two lingering issues, so Jack arranged for Amante to meet Simone for lunch, booking a second reservation to set Penny up with Fenix, the music producer he'd found in the grotto.

Jack's network effects quickly blossomed. Simone agreed to host Amante's non-fiction debut as the opening event at her politico-artistic penthouse, officially named The Turf, a dog-whistle landmine awaiting the club-foot steps of the gender-confused. The radical exclusion was made even more pointed by the open invitation of a "based" crossdresser whom all the conservative guys liked to pretend they didn't want to ravage from behind. In fact, some of them had done just that, followed by dramatic pleas not to tell their friends, their discreet Eskimo brethren, a fluid bond of secrecy among the new-wave right-wing.

Fenix agreed to bring Penny under his seasoned studio wing once he returned to New York, after an upcoming tour of South Africa playing hand percussion for a late-sprouting garage-revival five-piece. In other words, Jack earned his keep and intended to reap, mastering The Connector's subtle tradecraft, a sham of lazy brokerage when seen through the aperture of nescience. Penny returned to him uptown with earnest appreciation and a stay-bag full of clothes and an earworm to sing: a frizzy, forgotten '70s icon crooning shamanic, aquatic elegies for the warlock who owns her heart.

Jack subsidized the life of the party that spring, bars every night of the week like they'd been hired to pour drinks, burning cash as a blessèd offering to alcohol, the reality eater. Flower girls walking the aisle at weddings could net higher wages, plus benefits, and Penny's infinitesimal pay for pairing purple lisianthus with orange carnations barely covered the metro fare and energy drinks needed to work. He even kicked in eight hundred bucks for her rent, a room in a flophouse with antagonistic and delusional lesbian co-leasers, gals who made banal chitchat without gazing past their screens then charged you via Venmo for emotional labor. The space sat unused, devoid of decor, a few earthly belongings in the closet or on the floor. Financial desperation affected the smallest details of her day, including the need to use a radioactive green makeup palette inspired by a painful legal drama about lady superheroes, a gift from an out-of-touch family friend who thought she was a fan because "all girls your age need good role models"—thanks, Mrs. Stein!

Penny applied concealer and lipstick in Jack's narrow Manhattan bathroom. He explained, between labored coughs, his two- or three-pronged relationship with Ezekiel, who had come back to town incognito to attend Amante's book launch, apparently not hearing his fill of her upper-crust queenshit or garnering enough of a grope the last time they had sat together.

"Why would he subject himself to her concupiscence again?"

"Ask him yourself, we're about to meet for cheap cocktails."

Jack introduced Penny to his pseudo-mentor after they slid into a red vinyl booth at a converted diner up towards Harlem.

"Why would you subject yourself to Amante's concupiscence again?"

"Your conniving boyfriend tipped me off about *Amantellamonies*, his push for her to invest in the art scene, so I thought I'd brave the pit of despair between her legs once more, to dip my beak and profit."

Zeke and Penny liked each other in an instant, Jericho's horn blown to raze the walls of small-talk: The Connector strikes again.

"Jack told me about your music. Haven't listened, of course, but that's neat you do that."

She could banter, even while standing on the border of condescension. "You don't need to seek out my music, it will be on the radio, you'll be forced to listen, *everyone* will be forced to tune in, everyone will be compelled to worship God through song once theocratic monarchy is installed."

Zeke groaned. "Not you too!" He turned to Jack. "Let's refresh our drinks at the bar."

The two men drummed their fingers on the countertop, waiting for the mixologist to finish macking on two Finnish girls in paisley bucket hats.

"Your squeeze is nice."

Jack came clean on his obsession, its mutuality, how she had organized a party in his honor, the whole shebang. "It's like I've never made a mistake in romance, this is the ultimate fresh start."

Back at the table, they found Penny with her hands folded around a slender volume, bound with leather.

"Ah, a bookworm, what are you reading there?"

"It's for prayer, I try to embrace downtime without losing my soul to a phone."

Zeke laughed. "I haven't met any of these tradcaths yet, we don't have all that out in LA."

Ezekiel, broke as a bike spoke, struck a bargain to crash on Jack's roommate's couch the next couple of nights: free taxi rides and blow in exchange for the makeshift bed, an arrangement that dragged the trio into a confrontation with a whining Timothy and his stoned friends intending to watch the basketball game.

"He's only sleeping here, sports and sleep happen at drastically different hours."

"This apartment is too small for this many people, this isn't the deal I made with my buddy, it's not fair."

"Well part of being big and grown is rolling with the punches."

Perhaps there was a mild intimation of violence whenever one used the word "punches." This reminded Jack of a chick from the South who had relinquished her finger guns, a physical tic when cracking an unfunny joke, because she didn't want to be perceived as aggressive. She had a mohawk and black knuckles and multiple chains and couldn't have been less punk.

Jack almost condemned Timothy to death after realizing his boys were referring to a *fictional* basketball match-up, in a video game. Penny pulled an acoustic guitar off the wall and strummed a little ditty, the dust on the strings providing a pleasingly dirty tone that a lesser artist might fork out thousands to achieve in post-processing. The tension dissipated, and Zeke took off to meet a rising pianist in need of a booking agent. He promised to relink with the young infatuados downtown at The Turf for the launch. Penny called Gwen and convinced her to bring some available girlfriends to the event, "it will be a killer occasion to stunt on the sheltered and the homeschooled."

Jack and his chief lieutenants powwowed with the new gals of this sprouting harem—April, paralegal; May, secretary; and June, caregiver—at a scene bar sticky with the fragrance of sandalwood, a crater in the cement where the bouncer once ejected some bum for digging in his shorts for a stool sample. A plaque on the far wall acknowledged not one but two betrothments. The ladies assembled for a fast, frank pep speech from Captain Valentine.

"This party is exclusive, a meeting of the hyperonline pseudonyms, their investors, and the burgeoning intelligentsia of the counterculture, maybe even a couple actual artists. If you can't find a husband, at least bring back some leads."

He knew not the door policy of this first blowout, but a man who came bearing the gift of sociable women learned each and every whispered truth of the evening. Jack was double-dipping with this *kluge* (Yiddish phrase for three or more Jews pleased after a business deal). Broads bought access, access bought knowledge, knowledge bought power, a.k.a. additional clout, the semi-worthless coin of the realm.

Penny threaded her arm through his, a dignified couple leading the pack to Simone's penthouse. He felt like a chaste pimp, a pin-up pinball savant, The Who meets Hugh Hefner of the promised land. Outside the SoHo apartment building, his fluffle intermingled with a swarm of Young Republican types, sharply clothed in suits of plaid and khaki. Spirited conversation about tight immigration was met with feminine head nods and the catchphrases of active listening:

"Yep."

"Mmhm."

"I see."

"Go on."

Jack addressed the portly guard. "Valentine, plus five."

He perused the guestlist on his phone, marked the proper name, and escorted them to the private elevator. Titanium doors, activated with the proper keystrokes, opened up into a wood-paneled hall. Exposed rafters overshadowed a handful of folding chairs and seven pizza boxes of origins bourgeois. Spotless skylights illuminated an empty space loaded with autists, milling about like bumper cars. Attendants near the entrance distributed red tic-tacs in dimebags. Jack unleashed his harem to work the room and donned his mayor's hat to do the same, shaking hands either familiar or important. People smoked imported cigarettes with Ezekiel on an alabaster balcony, save for one microceleb relishing her permission to puff indoors. The pockets of awkward activity were punctuated by catty cliques, content to size up your drip or glance over your socials before engaging, mean girls roleplaying as thought-leaders. An oaf of a henchman, one master of bavardage who looked like a distended corpse floating in the surf post-shipwreck, bumbled from lunch table to lunch table, bridging gaps between preps and goths and geeks and jocks.

Near the speaker's lectern stood Amante, conspiring with Simone, both presiding over a stack of chunky tomes, freshly printed: *MAGNAnimous Mockery: Dissertations in Favor of Abso-Mon*. The motive for stringing together thousand-point Scrabble terms only to conclude with a clumsy, Jamaican-coded *patois-manteau*, well, guesses would be collected before the deep-dish was served.

Jack swallowed the pending bullet and sauntered towards the dynamic duo of doom to say his hellos and peruse the products.

"Gee Amante, how'd you find the time to compile and copyedit this whole collection?"

He flipped through heavy cream pages interspersed with QR code footnotes, digital stains leading to relevant clips and musical fragments from M. Carta cabaret, published and hosted at a newly-minted .uk web address.

"Puta, did you bring any more journalists to see my remarks?"

Jack lied through his gappèd teeth about the serviceable entourage of April, May, and June. "There are efforts afoot, Amante. I enlisted three assistants from prominent industries to survey the scene in shorthand, then report back to their respective bosses."

Simone offered reams of sickening chuckles. "She's like your sugar mama."

The closest Jack had ever come to snagging a verified paypig MILF was the night he drove over an hour to spend time with a menopausal gas station manager he met online while lying about his age. She let him pump for free, screaming "there's no way you're only twenty-nine makin' me feel this good." Jack had barely been twenty-three.

Penny passed Jack a business card, given to her in exchange for a sweet smile. Free champagne flowed. An undercover federal agent, a snitch with no stitch and the girliest voice imaginable, tried to blend in, pecking the cheek of his unconvincing lady-partner. A scrappy blonde climbed the ceiling's support beams, a five-foot-nothing duppy plastered on gypsum and lime, her once-beautiful face bloated from the second-order effects of schnapps.

"Pick-me's be crazy."

"Here comes the queen of 'em," Jack added.

Amante stepped to the podium to greet the slacking crowd, a council of silent professors assembled in a semicircle behind her.

"Are those contributors or bodyguards?"

Amante waited for the chatter to die down, then kept waiting after the room turned stoic, all those assembled anticipating some profound Book of Revelation prophecy on the future of American governance.

Simone made an announcement. "The floor is open for questions."

Without context or introduction provided by the stage, the Q&A began life as a legal deposition, dry inquiries establishing basic facts about the case.

"What's your name?"

"Amante."

"What's your last name?"

"I won't be answering that at this time."

Exhausted by the dull proceedings, Jack scribbled a prompt and passed it to Gwen.

"Why like, tear down the Magnum Cartridge?"

His handwriting: hieroglyphic chicken-scratch. Gwen continued, off-book.

"Why not frame your campaign with a positive message, people love the Royal Family for example, they might support you if you talk about them, it's like hiding the mass death of children behind the word pro-choice..."

Amante avoided the rambling inquiry with a non-sequitur, an attempt at humor, an alien form observing the human condition, studied yet never directly experienced.

"Well, there are forty-two synonyms for ignorance..."

Her cronies erupted with hilarity, mystifying the audience. She held up a copy of her essay collection, a high priestess consecrating a heedless congregation that grew more rowdy by the minute.

"How do you feel about your book as a versatile object? Doorstop, booster seat, six months worth of kindling once the empire falls," asked a bold naysayer from the wings, garnering a proper laugh from the audience.

Amante replied with unassailable fury, the likes of which Jack had never seen directed at him despite many missteps.

"It could even be used as a blunt weapon to demolish the skulls of the opposition! The pen is mightier than the sword, and the book is heavier than the bomb!"

Penny bravely tried to sway the crowd towards truth in spite of the speaker's purchased power.

"What about an alliance with Catholic strength and competency in pursuit of *theocratic* monarchy? Moral degradation in the abstract garners many enemies."

Amante's rage bubbled over, a cauldron of bitter resentment with an ex-husband's infidelities as the bouillon, having left her at the kitchen island to chase the modest skirts of a parochial schoolgirl.

"I reject the assumed inherent righteousness of Church leadership, especially given their gentle attitude towards pedophiles. We are proposing a different strain of reactionary politics, a vanguard borne from an interrupted lineage. In the spirit of transformative change, I'm marking this special occasion with the announcement of my charitable grant program, *Amantellamonies*. Funds will be awarded to creative projects that antagonize the tenets of representative democracy in creative ways. Copies of *MAGNAnimous Mockery: Dissertations in Favor of Abso-Mon* sold at this event include instructions on how to submit proposals."

The attendees applauded in a frenzy. Amante fled the scene, happy to organize without needing to carouse. Dissent dissipated in a flash of fash; everyone was on the payroll now.

"Did you know that was about to happen?" Penny said with some trepidation.

"It was my idea, right down to the name. She'll probably head home and open negotiations with Pope Francis after that contrived rebuttal."

The mob descended on the merchandise table, swearing their allegiance with the swipe of a card in hopes of securing Amante's patronage, tearing the last book in two, knowledge devoured, resorting to the reach of their fists to settle the matter of ownership.

"Fucking braindead barbarians." Ezekiel dumped cocaine on Jack's hand to distribute to the girls, who gummed low doses after sharing their social successes: April had met a guy in publishing, May had met a guy in banking, and June had met a guy in town from Hollywood, all three doling out contact info to their handler in exchange for the powder. Gwen demurred, citing work in the morning.

Security loosened, and a few blacktivists snuck around canvassing for signatures to defeat, or support, some provincial referendum in Bronx politics, fielding disdainful stares from the majority and the attention of a philosophy minor, who baited them into a wry debate on human biodiversity. They shortly realized they had rapped upon the wrong chamber door. There's that scrappy blonde again, beating her cheating boyfriend with the thick textbook of *beau monde* babble.

Penny and Jack retreated into the alcove. She licked the drugs from his fingers, her rate-of-speech tripling while she ranted about Amante's predictable response to theological rule.

"Husbands should be prepared to defend their wives against such things."

That wasn't really Jack's best mode, preferring to accumulate data before diving into an argument, for fear of fluster and insults hurled in the face of one-time interlocutors. More disco hits filled the penthouse, safe crowd-pleasers in spite of everyone's proud position as self-described radicals.

With concessions made for the obligatory run of social engagements expected of minor cultural dignitaries, their newfound brood of acquaintances reading and screening and screaming across downtown Manhattan, Penny and Jack continued to pass large portions of night and day facing each other, nursing the shared delusion that fates misaligned would stave off the grave.

Unable to wrestle the common room's TV set from addicted-gamer Timothy—denigrating his distant friends' mothers on teamspeak 'til the witching hour—Jack roped Penny into a fishing trip at an upscale hotel bar with an unassuming name in Midtown; she would serve as tantalizing bait to hook a benefactor.

"If any of these septuagenarians like what they see, a couple polite dates is all it takes, they have ED, just a closed-mouth smooch and they'll cough up the cash for studio time."

"This old sculptor in Ohio once asked to marry me."

"So you know the drill then. If this works, I could become your promoter full-time."

"You mean my pimp? I think you have me confused with one of your other whores."

"I should sit across the room, I'm scaring off potential suitors."

She stopped him in his tracks with a gentle hand on the arm. "Is this your brilliant idea for a sweet date?"

"We spend every moment together, waking or otherwise, we don't need to go on dates."

Ten minutes passed without interest or incident, and Penny lured him back. "My namesake during confirmation was Saint Agnes. Men who tried to rape her were struck blind."

"Why did you pick her?"

"She chose me." A devious smile. "Her greatest enemy, the ones she hoped would burn, were sodomites and various other disordered fornicators."

Penny's angelic nature appeared before him, on that first frosted evening in January, as a shining silhouette among the clouds, with information since then suggesting that the silver linings obscured dark, demented details, the vague impression of a sex-obsessed past. He despised the image, picturing her sucking and fucking a queue of eager guys. What had made her turn to religion anyway? A hard reset after a period of utter sluttery? Too many rides on the cock carousel? College girls liked to wear out their holes "finding themselves" before settling down with Mr. Right, withered husks by the age of twenty-two.

"What about you, what led you to become a Christian heretic?"

"I grew up in a home surrounded by Hallmark word-art strewn across the wall, live-laugh-love signifiers of affection, missing the real thing. It was all very pomo, ripping the family apart to snap a photo of a Happy Family, everyone forced to submit to unreality. Threats of eyes and ears everywhere to ensure good behavior."

Penny laughed, reading from a different script. "That's so Protestant."

"The narcissism of small differences," Jack said.

She stroked his face. "You're a pilgrim, an extraterrestrial, not of this world. I'm sorry you landed in the wrong family."

Jack and Penny returned to an empty apartment. He showed her a mournful ballad, a songwriter commemorating the demise of Van Gogh, a beautiful death on a pedestal. She reimagined the music as an incel anthem, "perhaps they'll listen now" delivered with the enormous, you'll-all-see pupils of a mass shooter. When she excused herself to the restroom, he couldn't help but snoop in her email; he rolled his eyes and unsubscribed her from CatholicMatch.com.

The rapturous moment arrived, and Jack could no longer avoid tagging along to Mass; his well of excuses run dry, his trail of overlapping plans paved over, he reluctantly donned the uniform of belief and prepared to submit beneath the bell tower on that most holy of days, Easter Sunday.

"I'm one year old," she proclaimed without a trace of irony, intending to celebrate her birthday in the faith with another DIY concert that evening.

Jack started his morning at the parade grounds of a middle Brooklyn park, a hell of a train ride from uptown for a pick-up game of touch football, organized biweekly between journalists writing for rival outlets on the sociopolitical beat. The teams were picked fresh each time but more or less aligned along the axis of Progressives vs. Reactionaries. That weekend also coincided with Passover, so the match became the Abrahamic Bowl, Christians vs. Jews. The weird Buddhist reporter and his Sikh friend were encouraged to stay home and rest, while the Muslims were mid-fast and made for weak opponents on the pitch.

After the game, Jack bussed up to Ridgewood, a slow-to-gentrify haven for anarchists proud to have the death tally of the nineteenth-century Paris commune inscribed on their moleskin ledgers, LARPers with cheap rent and red string tied around their necks. Gwen lived over this way in an apartment sharing a border with Queens, and an assemblage of oddballs were gathering for a He-is-risen feast in advance of the church service that afternoon.

Penny, mojito in tow, embraced Jack with a three-second kiss. "It makes me so happy that you're finally going to church. God is working overtime in our lives. Our ship is coming in!"

With the holiday double bill and the open minds of post-Bushwick party hosts, several Hebrews joined the festivities in order to feel oppressed by prayer, casting uncanny looks at each other when Penny praised the one true God. Jack found the practice of getting tanked before worship a little odd, but then again he was encountering a different sect here. The COEXIST delegation gnashed their teeth on mashed potatoes, and Jack grabbed Penny to lay with him on the couch in a loving stupor. She wore a magnificent white dress, "so everyone can see my purity." He nuzzled into the nape of her neck, fielding criticism from Gwen across the room.

"Let's keep those hands in sight above the blanket."

Jack chuckled. "This is just Grandpa's tradition every year after Easter lunch."

The hosanna caravana split off from the Semites and hitched a ride across the river to Nolita for the vigil service. On the brief walk from metro station to cathedral, an anti-miracle from outer heaven fell upon Jack's furrowed forehead, the foul filth of a passing pigeon smudging his sunglasses, an omen for Penny to heed, turn, and run. She saw the sign and ignored its implications, locking herself in a café bathroom to cleanse the waste from his face.

"You are so beautiful, so striking, such a man," she said, wet washcloth in hand, dabbing at the birdshit.

Gwen knocked like a disciplinarian and the gang scurried to the service, finding seats among the rear pews with the other youth. Families lurked near the eaves in case the need arose for a quick split: babies, ready to explode into tears, were handed back and forth between parents, taking turns to kneel. Displeased and stoic, Jack flashed to the teeth-pulling of church as a child, his only prayer offered to the patron saint of sleep to intercede when his folks came to wake him, beg thy mother and father for mercy from another hour of bible study. He should have dosed himself with an edible post-lunch, all the better to enjoy mouthing the word "watermelon" while his brothers-and-sisters-in-Christ raised the slippery melody of their voices in glorious exultation. He caught the eye of many a mildly familiar scenester seen or spoken to at events that season; were all these cokeheads confessing their habits or skipping the booth?

The time for transubstantiation was nigh, and the population assumed the position of reverence while the priest blessed the Body and the Blood. Jack's ex, Violet, once fed the little wafers to drunk party guests; Jack's story unfolded first as farce, *then* as a most serious affair. He wanted to receive communion, his spirit buzzed with the energy of the mass of believers congregating under one roof, but Penny insisted he linger behind at their seats.

"You haven't earned it yet."

If Jesus died for the sins of all, why the need to jump through hoops and bark on command for a little wine? And how come these people chop off the Lord's Prayer after the line about evil and deliverance?

"I love you," she whispered.

"I love you too. This is great, you're basically my wife already."

She grew stiff. "It's a lot more complicated than that."

Jack took the comment in stride, and the parishioners of that Irish basilica humbly cried "amen." After parting ways with Penny—she heading off to sound check for the show, he fleeing with a mumbled alibi about needing a breather and a reassurance not to be tardy—he rambled around the west-side docks, in secular torment over the eidolon in his mind's eye: to teach a child to feel guilt over the Earth's turning was to fail as a parent. The young and curious ached for real answers to their idle inquiries instead of "them's the rules" or "I said so" or "God's will be done," punting the toughest talks to a heavenly father in a blame game rather than forking over practical advice. When he was a boy, his indigo intuition had stirred up specific questions, namely how an all-powerful, ever-present entity could possibly decide *not* to extinguish the Demiurge, the evils hiding in the cracks: "Why won't the Lord smite the Taliban" and "How come kids in Africa are hungry" and so on. He received no satisfactory counsel from his parents or pastors. His resolve had crystallized: after escaping the civilization-ending trend of healthy adults opting to forgo offspring, he swore to enact a detached policy of ontology, a vast second-floor library where sons and daughters could choose their own adventures through the literary and the philosophical.

Would Penny abide? Out of the cesspool of women populating his bodycount, and the handful who'd avoided the ledger through rejection or friendship, she was the first who seemed poised to conquer the neuroses which prevented one from becoming a competent mother. An adman at a heterodox firm had recently told him that "raising children with religion is the ultimate gift"—a statement of cope from

134

an atheistic, ancestral Jew, but also the only upbringing Jack had known, his free will permitting the retreat from belief. Christianity was the European default throughout the Dark Ages; maybe the twenty-first century of the selfie had produced a paradox of choice, the potential to stray and seek fulfillment from material goods, to-go boxes instead of family dinners, fandom instead of community, high rents instead of homesteading, furbabies instead of white picket fences, *Two and a Half Men* instead of 2.5 kids.

His thinking suffered, a lack of color or clarity, a millstone 'round the neck in moments of strife that could beckon him off the roof of a six-story building if left unchecked, the drive to obliterate when unable to penetrate the mackerel sky around his grey matter. Faced with the frothing spray of the Hudson, he threw off the yoke of the chewed-cud loop and hurried to see Penny perform in the locker room of a crêpe parlor, the fourth venue booked by sloppy organizers who couldn't deliver a down payment in a timely manner, yet insisted on a rider with specific terms about three-point lighting and blackout curtains and complementary nutritious snacks.

The boyfriend of the evening's soubrette, Jack expected list privileges, hyping himself up for a persuasive interaction at the door only to fall upon a vacated folding chair and a plastic soup dish with scribbled label: DONATIONS 4 TALLENT. With all his geese as swans, he proceeded past diners munching on sweet and savory French treats, descending a dim staircase lined with flyers for some "Pussy Grabs Back" Queer Arts Showcase, a pogrom for his ilk, following the call of the bass rebounding from the basement.

There was no stage, a comedian's nightmare, no elevation above the crowd to imply a hierarchy between doer and viewer. There wasn't much of an audience either, a casualty of confusion from the constant stream of location changes, potential cheerleaders stranded across the two primary boroughs for culture, barking up former trees then requesting back their hard-earned sap. Jack's presence added five to ten percent of the total headcount. He arrived mid-act to witness a slender nubian princess, lip-syncing to autotuned tracks with her galligaskins piled around her ankles, repetitive lyrics encouraging the listener to "do *you*" and "be *gay*" scored by bubble-gum smacking beats and the swivel of Brazilian-waxed hunkers *in puris naturalibus*. He settled in next to a churlish Penny, arms crossed, face frozen with a frown.

"What's this unholy travesty? On Easter Sunday, of all days. Are you playing next?"

She beckoned him to join her in the smoking section, a below-ground alleyway with a miniscule, mightily-distant rectangle of open ozone above, and explained that her adolescent instrumentalist was MIA and incommunicado by telephone.

"He's not even thirteen, what could he possibly be doing instead of backing you up on the six-string?"

"That boy is a buffoon. He'll never make it in this town. Why are you so late?"

Jack begged off with a line about stretching his legs, then fed her half a Vyvanse to bolster her mood. "You don't need his juvenile twangs, sing them Uncle K. acapella."

Gwen popped her head out of the hatch. "That loose fish bitch is finished."

Jack inhaled his cigarette in a single puff and returned inside. Penny stepped behind the mic. With tight embouchure and her masculine muse as visible support, she enraptured the tiny assembly, an anthem for the falsely-imprisoned Unabomber stunning the layabouts into silence. A few were quick to congratulate her once the reverb faded; others returned to their fool's paradise. Jack planted his dense caveman brow on her elegant forehead, bonking with a grin.

"If I cracked open both our loafs like nuts, we could always be on each other's minds."

"Has anyone ever told you that you're like catnip for BPD girls?"

The Manhattan Order of Streetwise Mendicants—when not preoccupied with the hustle for alms—were quick to offer unsolicited wisdom on affairs of the heart, often overhearing wistful laments about loneliness in this atomized, transplant-laden city, and interjecting with a bracing "THEN GO THE FUCK HOME THEN!" Loud chatter attracted them like pests to crumbs, but even a certain gait in the step could solicit uninvited commentary. In lieu of ten fingers, half his and half hers, intertwined on a morning stroll around Morningside, Jack caressed the nape of Penny's neck, firm grip denoting both loving care and control over their route.

A guy in tattered rags shouted his advice while scavenging in a trash can. "Hey man, quit grabbing that lady like that, you tryna choke a chick out or something?"

Jack stretched his arm further, a defiant headlock, glancing back with "don't tell me what to do" eyes and a "go play on the freeway" smirk.

Penny rubbed her cheek against his sleeve. "Doesn't he know all girls are cats? You're keeping me safe from dogs."

"He certainly howled about it, the vagrant hound." Jack leaned in close. "Maybe we should acquire a leash, so I can walk my kitten around the block in peace."

"I'm not really into that kind of stuff anymore."

Jack sulked the whole way home, skull circled by kinky crows. His ex Charlotte, the Queen of Infant Death, had a checklist, every known fetish and even a few fabricated, which she furnished for aspiring sexual partners to complete with enthusiasm, marking either "Big Fan," "Somewhat Curious," or "Not For Me" on hair pulling, piss play, gangbangs, and far too much more, corny transactional fornication rendered a higher level of mundane through injections of liquid bureaucracy, like dousing tempeh with steak sauce. She carried her spreader bar and leather straps and ball gag in an "I'm With Her" tote bag.

Once Penny crossed the apartment's threshold, Jack gave her a taste of his stewing thoughts. "Why do I feel like I missed out on your most lively era?" He expressed his desire for her in point-blank terms, his will to dominate, to feel and fill her flesh.

"All the regulations are gay, most of those power dynamics are baked in, it's contraceptive to make a lifestyle out of it," Penny countered.

"But I want to have fun with you, adult fun."

"You want to have your cake and eat it too."

"That expression never made sense to me, what else are you supposed to do with cake?"

"I told you once before, I'm not here to have fun." Penny explained her pursuit of the divine, how it's never too late to strive for sainthood.

"Where was this holy attitude when you were being leashed and bound by your ex?"

She grew morose, telling Jack about her former live-in boyfriend, how straightforward lovemaking no longer satisfied.

"He said he wanted more out of me."

A night of shoulder-shaking sobs had been followed by a day of research, the borderliner's need to please. She compiled a list of sadomasochistic tactics to earn her place back in his black heart.

"That's awful." Jack suppressed the urge to ask for explicit details, to discover the specific activities they did together and lament the fact that he wouldn't get a piece of the action.

Emboldened by the dirty discussion and entitled to enact psychosexual praxis, Jack kissed a crescent moon across her tight belly, winding lips and tongue 'round hips until she couldn't handle the sensation, pulling his fingers towards the moist area between her legs.

"Feel what you do to me and know that I want nothing more than to be with you."

He buried his face inside until her spine arched with orgasm, her first in over a year. She returned the courtesy in a flurry of passion and took him fully down her throat, the hypersensitive cannon prematurely firing its payload.

She wiped her mouth. "Sperm brain makes that tolerable, it's mind control for women."

His laugh was hijacked by a brutal coughing fit and a searing pain in his right side, the muscles straining for relief, every additional expulsion of air a genocide for the cells in his lungs.

"We're being punished for shattering each other's chastity," she said.

"Something serious," he wheezed, "is wrong with my insides, need hospital now."

An elite medical school lay a few blocks to the north, and Jack limped in that direction, supported by Penny's fragile figure, his organs screaming. She seemed aloof, referencing the stigmata, the wound in the right flank of Jesus Christ, his perfect skin pierced by a soldier's lance, the Spear of Destiny later wielded by Hitler, esoteric means for tyrannical ends—imparting little concern over Jack's health in the here and now.

"Your bones are numbered too."

Religious ecstasy is common in schizophrenics; of course a society that worships false idols would lock away the clear-eyed and beatified.

Jack checked in at the hospital through clenched teeth. Penny continued to perfume herself with the odor of sanctity, scorning the trend of Clown Mass, priests dressed as pro wrestlers consecrating potato chips. He slumped next to her in the plastic hardback playplace chairs. A woman at the remote end of the reception area retched into a wastebasket, cleaning her mouth with the cloth mask on her chin.

"Why must the global leaders in reverence stoop low and change with the times," Penny said to no one in particular.

Jack prepped a lecture on that law of conquest, something about institutions naturally progressing politically unless specifically dedicated to the conservation of values, but remained silent, the act of speech stifled by inflamed windpipes. Escorted to an examination room by a nurse, Jack crumpled on the hospital bed, his too-small faded-blue floral-print shirt lifting to reveal pale skin.

"The sunless shade of quality genes," Penny informed him while clutching his hand.

A handsome giant of a medical professional, biceps bulging through his scrubs, marched into the room to check on Jack, towering over the frail boy on the antiseptic cot. Preliminary questions were asked and answered: how hurt, how much, how long.

"Your lungs sound pristine," the man said from the operator's end of a stethoscope.

"I think my apartment is killing me." Jack withheld the intolerable amount of cigarettes smoked weekly from his chart.

Unable to determine a cause apart from the psychosomatic, the doctor nevertheless diagnosed him with one pulled external oblique, prescribing pain-relief benzocaine patches and a cough suppressant to prevent the strain from growing worse.

"I'm sure your sister here will take great care of you," the strapping physician said, winking at Penny on his way out the door.

Jack slipped his patient bracelet onto her slender wrist. "Mental hospital marriage."

"That doctor looked exactly like one of my exes."

Filled with visions of her perfect breasts pressed against the thighs of some massive b-ball titan, Jack crafted his cruel response with intent to maim.

"That's funny because you look like two of my favorite exes, fused together into a greater whole through the miracle of science."

The last bit, a backhanded compliment, served as a smokescreen of plausible deniability; Penny sulked the whole way home all the same, unable to traverse the moat of mope circling her heart. On the couch, his cough returned with vigor, a stint on the inquisitor's rack.

"I can't spend another minute in this subleased deathtrap," he moaned, scrolling on his laptop, a search query for "cheap activities NYC" offering few suggestions, mostly museums, pay-what-you-wish for residents, their girthy fiscal endowments covering the difference.

During the Rockefeller family's front-page prominence, a vintage culture war was afoot, competing animus, the early inklings of artistic institutions repurposed for the tasteless general population driving the ultra-rich to revolt. Their preference, for a private club to safekeep collected paintings and host campestrian galas, lost to *vox populi*. One of that rock 'n' roll fella's heirs cared deeply for the preservation of medieval pieces, in a monastic locus way up yonder in Washington Heights, a journey that Jack pitched to his pious girlfriend.

"If we left now, and I need to, we could enjoy a couple hours of spiritually-nourishing art before the sun sets."

Penny looked grim, unexcitable even at the prospect of this Catholic-adjacent pastime. "I'd like to go to confession before entering such a holy place."

"Did you hear me? We have a limited window of time, and even this far uptown it will take us an hour on the train."

"I'm in a state of mortal sin."

"It's not like we had sex, since when does hand 'n' mouth stuff count," he argued with the logic of a high-school boy.

"I'd prefer to stand before paintings and carvings of Christ with a clean soul and settled conscience."

"I'm still so damned fuzzy on the reason for your conversion, what with all that babble about St. Agnes' crusade against sodomy, your hang-ups over physical intimacy. I feel like you're burying history as a whore."

With some reluctance, she recounted the fallout after her Big Breakup, lost and abandoned and hopeless, a period of rampant casual sex—"by my trad monogamous standards"— that obviously failed to fill the empty glass. Jack's attention faded in and out, a defensive measure against the curse of learning too much and soiling the Platonic ideal. He caught a tidbit about Penny sweating bullets, consumed with intrusive sexual ideation beneath the glare of the suspended crucifix. Female desire was a fickle device, their yen for men opaque and misleading when applied to anyone other than the current object of interest.

"I've shared this story dozens of times while converting, for some reason I'm finding it hard to tell you..." She trailed off, caught between heavenly host, father son and holy ghost, and the skeptical love of her young life.

Jack dragged a pouting Penny north through Fort Tryon Park, green expanses full of the jobless and the elderly and families on spring break, a communal pilgrimage to the stonecraft of an imitation abbey, a simulacrum of devotion constructed from the building blocks of consecrated ruins pillaged from the old country.

After ascending three staircases and as many switchbacks then forking over a buck apiece to the disinterested clerk, the quietly feuding couple stood in awe of the stained-glass Jesuit hegemony, the promised Prince of Peace in a swirl of esoteric imagery cobbled together from both pagan and Hebrew iconography, levitating at the end of chronological time.

"If I'm not meant to succeed with music, maybe I should join a convent, my tatters of dignity restored as a novice of the sisterhood."

Jack chose irreverence, referencing the nunsploitation of a favorite film about God's gals, horny and depraved in a state of orgiastic frenzy under the influence of "witchcraft," a cynical hoax to help seize control of a town from a politically-inconvenient priest, enacted through hangings and burnings, enemas full of boiling water and a spiked Spanish boot.

Penny ignored her grating boyfriend and stepped into a hall packed with glass display cases of manuscript illuminations. Oversized ornate letters hosted hand-drawn peasants, partying on the page and leering at the words. Jack spotted a fair farmgirl tending to a despicable imp with one arm and cartoonish tufts of hair.

Deeper in the crypt of New Jerusalem, Jack was struck by the potency of Christ: lying in the wings of life were far worse fates than the rich tradition of Catholic faith, to set aside his vulgarity and antagonism, to lean in and accrue benefits, the mystic power of mass belief to move mountains, or at least reduce them to anthills...what was he protecting with such ferocity, so much poisoned alacrity?

Sleep brought the kind of peace only available on the Stygian shore, temporary reprieve from the sharp spasms of spiritual sickness, and silent convalescence from the woes of troubled love.

Jack prepared breakfast, two bowls of muesli and milk delivered bedside. The pain of a coughing fit exploded once more in his chest, yet the food in his hands remained intact, unspilled, his sense of humor preserved as a side dish akin to fried bacon or roasted potatoes.

"I recently tried my hand at penning short fiction." Jack began to read from his spiral notebook, the discount price-tag still on the cover.

In rebellion against the perceived bondage of his upbringing, Jimmy Harper had spent nearly a decade of adulthood on the lam from Christianity, organized or otherwise. His pseudo-spiritual, stand-for-nothing-fall-for-anything disposition in the interim had dragged him along paths which skirted internet atheism, pagan goddess-worship, Arab mysticism, and even the deification of comic book strongmen. He had never dabbled in the Jewish arts, though a few slim, rare volumes of *Kabbalah for Knuckleheads* continued to accrue value, unopened on his bookshelf. Fortunately, both for Jimmy and for his extended family of born-again prophets and heretical amputees back home in Tennessee, the abundance of modern cults running rampant across these amber waves of grain had failed to wrap their respective crooks around his neck, as the lapsed-Protestant Jimmy maintained a belief in the sovereignty of the

144

individual, illuminated by an unmediated relationship with a Higher Power, whatever and ever amen. Jimmy had also done time—just a lil' spell—in a program for recovering alcoholics, though the road away from the school of hard-hittin' liquor proved much longer than a twelve-step stretch of country highway.

His saving grace, a supernatural gift bearing gilded hair ties instead of yuletide boughs, came in the form of a girl named Sharlene Dixon, a docile beauty with high-falutin' aspirations to live a more painterly life, a conclusion she had drawn after a bus trip from Appalachia to the big city of Chicago, wherein the austere imagination of Edward Hopper's *Nighthawks* struck her raw right where she stood. Sharlene had bought a pair of socks depicting the masterpiece from the museum's store and, despite quickly ripping an unmendable hole in one, the other covered her left foot the night that hick love emerged after meeting sweet Jimmy at the last 24/7 diner in her town.

"I'm just passing through ma'am, though I'd sure-as-sugar do it again if it meant I could take you out drivin.'"

Sharlene beamed. "You askin' me on a date, Mister Man?"

Jimmy wrapped his big hand 'round her little finger. "I'm requestin' your company as my co-pilot."

Sharlene thought Jimmy sounded educated and romantic, that being the last thought that crossed her mind before she found herself seated shotgun in a souped-up Cadillac pushing ninety out on them roads under cover of darkness.

Thrilled by the speed, Sharlene flirted, "If I was the type to lay with a stranger, this would definitely get me goin.'"

"Sorry to disappoint ma'am, but I've been chaste for about two months now."

"Is that so?" she sang in, well, a sing-song voice.

"Maybe one-and-a-half." Jimmy winked.

Before parting ways on that first occasion, Jimmy swept Sharlene off her fine-art souvenir feet with a deep kiss on the mouth.

Their second date found Jimmy and Sharlene investigating the local carnival, striped tent-tops standing tall against the jaundiced trees of late autumn as though someone had flipped a consignment shirt sideways. On their lazy stroll around the midway, Sharlene expressed particular interest in a pink stuffed animal—a bear with unknowable, beady eyes—which Jimmy won in a pinch by pitching that perfect sphere of America's pastime through a too-narrow gap in the plywood wall of some former convict's traveling hovel.

"Seems like you earned yourself a mighty fine prize already," the carnie sneered in Sharlene's general direction. His words trailed off into the unpleasant wheeze of chronic obstructive pulmonary disease.

Renowned in certain social circles for an extraordinary temper and the bruised fists to prove it, Jimmy stuck with soft verbal menace. "Put them crooked eyes somewhere else."

The carnie wore an ill-fitting suit of stained khaki and harbored a mild death wish. "You're a lucky doll, trapped a college lad between your legs." He leered at Sharlene from hat to hoof.

Jimmy lost his cool and launched a second baseball down the lane of the ramshackle game. His aim was true once more, busting the fat nose of the man who spoke out of turn, scattering thin droplets of blood across the rest of the plush creatures.

The two courting birds took shelter in the carnival's mess hall and shared a mid-size platter of french fries. Sharlene was of two minds: on the one hand, she was flattered by the fact that a handsome hunk had defended her honor; on the other, she was terrified by such a naked display of violence.

"Do you worship the Lord above, Jimmy Harper?"

"Been 'round that wheel a few too many times." Jimmy lightened his tone. "I was baptized by a Pentecostal preacher with a fourteen-year-old wife and handguns hidden in Gideon Bibles. Call it disillusionment, call it shattered faith, but I ain't felt the spark of the divine since I was a lil' kid."

Touched by an intuitive feeling of his innate goodness, Sharlene laid a hand on his thigh. "I think you're one of us, one of the elect. I think my sweet Jimmy is part of the special club of folks gettin' to walk the pretty sidewalks in Heaven."

He looked at her blankly.

Sharlene continued, "it's called predestination." She pronounced it like some dirty word they'd kick you off the TV for muttering. "Jesus Christ suffered for us and us alone! Our salvation has been determined by his death!" In her frenzied excitement, Sharlene knocked over their plate of fries. She hugged the pink plush prize close to her chest and continued in hushed tones. "Don't'ya get it? Before God ever created the world, he chose you and me and people like us to be saved and live forever in paradise, just like you chose me and I chose you."

Jimmy squeezed in a comment. "What about sin? Don't it matter?"

"Best to start behaving like the good chosen people I know you are inside."

Jimmy smirked, content to be the object of her religious fixations. "You're so pretty, all passionate when you're talkin' and such."

Sharlene wrapped her arms around his reddish neck. "Won't you come along next time some of us elect get together? There's a lil' event comin' up next month. It'd be real nice if you joined me. Let's just take a train into town with an open mind and we'll be right as a cold rain."

Happy for the opportunity to please and strengthen their budding bond, Jimmy agreed to accompany Sharlene on her upcoming trip to Chicago.

Years ago, convention centers had replaced temples as the event horizon of mass belief. Prayer, pillaged by commerce, had established a legion of transnational conglomerate feast days on which weekend warriors, golf courtesans, jukebox heroes, and armchair enthusiasts of all flavors could gather for light bites and secular fellowship. Jimmy and Sharlene approached an imposing monolith that ripped a black hole in the skyline. She sported a reverent, grateful expression and dragged a roller suitcase.

"That's a big ol' bag for such a short trip."

Sharlene squeezed his arm. "I sure am glad to have you around to protect my fragility, Jimmy Harper."

"Let's see if my navigatin's as good as my protectin.'" Jimmy craned his neck, pretending not to see the massive glass complex in front of him, the largest repository for drink tickets and plastic badge casings in North America.

Sharlene grabbed his noggin and tilted it up towards their destination. "See anything?"

Jimmy simulated a look of surprise. "Could've missed it completely. What would I do without my co-pilot?"

Upon crossing the threshold of the convention center, Sharlene and Jimmy were greeted by a verified cornucopia of special-interest delights: Italian automobiles, German rock bands, Spanish pastry distributors, and a small sign off to the side that seemed to suggest French cobblers, shoes not sweets.

Sharlene pointed him towards the Francophile placard. Jimmy followed the directional arrows luring them into *L'Arche de Jean.*

Sharlene rubbed the back of Jimmy's neck, explaining, "Our host went all in on them translations a few years back. There were issues with protestors, nasty Communist Chinamen and their boring obedient wives, naysayers and nonbelievers who couldn't handle consenting adults gettin' together to debate doctrine and worship. Them Chinese people hate animals, that's why they eat dogs and rats. I grew up playin' in God's dirt, and munching on friendly beasts is too much even for me."

Jimmy ducked out of the flow of foot traffic to speak to Sharlene privately. "What's all this about God save the animals and what have you? And do you smell that? Like huffing permanent markers—"

Sharlene unzipped her suitcase from the wheel-end. "I need you to trust me, our connection don't work without a sprinkle of trust." She extracted two opaque garment bags. "Put this on and meet me inside. Don't forget the gloves."

A hulking brown bear stalked down the long, dim corridor to the special room marked *Jean's Ark*. The coordinators didn't bother with clever misdirection that deep inside the biggest business palace in all the land. With a paw around the aluminum door handle, the brown bear stumbled into the secret space for his kind.

He found all the familiar trappings of niche industry assembly—coffee samovars, printed pamphleture, branded step-and-repeat for photo ops beneath uncanny fluorescent beams—and yet, the attendees there appeared furrier. The brown bear spotted canines, felines and porcupines, plus kangaroos and lizards, too. Beside every animal was the incarnate form of its opposite number, a male and a female for each species. The drowsy brown bear yearned to reunite with his perfect match, feeling incomplete and alone among the unknown crowd.

A smaller, more-delicate paw intertwined with his. He spun around, barely discerning her shape through his mask: a pink bear, with eyes of pleasure.

"This one is new. I sewed it stitch by stitch, just for you."

The brown bear grumbled an unintelligible response.

"Thanks for coming with me. It means the world, and now we can inherit it."

The pink bear guided the brown bear to a pair of folding chairs by the main stage. A clinically-obese man with a staggering white beard, Kris Kringle reimagined as philosopher of antiquity, climbed the lectern to address the chosen faithful in scripted performance.

"Welcome all ye fated elect to *Jean's Ark* '23. Your presence all but guarantees your deliverance from the evils of society and the decline of our once-towering civilization."

The audience erupted into a frenzy of howls and growls, roars and more, the hysterical reverberations of jungle badlands nearing destruction.

"I'm incredibly excited to kick off this year's liturgical calendar with a dynamic afternoon of breakout sessions covering sovereignty, hierarchy, and animal husbandry."

The pink bear nuzzled against her brown bear. "That's where we learn 'bout how to get married to each other."

The brown bear, sedated, only managed a mild whimper.

The ancient actor announced that "true disciples fear nothing, neither discipline nor sadistic impulse, for fear is pesticide to profound contemplation. Those who know the applied difference may follow me into the backrooms."

Drawn along by a cosmic string, the brown bear trailed behind the heretical thespian towards a chamber of quadrupedal domination. The pink bear gazed on in horror at the twisted proceedings hidden from the view of general admission ticket-holders: a bacchanal of writhing figures and discarded feathers, farm critters in doggystyle and domestic pets locked within miniature barn stalls, leashes and leg snares and a rack of zoo-grade pharmaceutical tranquilizers along the wall, that inimitable impersonator of Jean Calvin presiding over all.

With heart blackened by the spirit of brutality, the brown bear abandoned his pink bride-to-be and entered the Boschian hellscape of bondage. He found an even-smaller white bear, either polar or bipolar. The larger, darker outsider unleashed the nine flails of an obsidian whip upon her fur-covered back, each pathetic yelp only encouraging him to beat her harder.

"I don't appreciate all that blasphemy and sacrilege."

"It's about Calvinists, not Catholics."

Jack and Penny lounged and listened to the Old Testament blues rock of crusty, crazy warhorses, rain beating away against the alleyway windowpane, then took a nap, extra rest to prepare for the week to come, dodging coughs and further temptation.

At a repurposed utility station in Midtown, a gallery show titled *A [Roman] Salute to Narcissism*: linoleum walls lined with bleak, pseudo-intellectual photography, second-angle shots documenting subjects in the midst of snapping vapid selfies, plus a video-art compilation of the same. The viewers sipped low-end white wine and nodded as if uncovering supreme human truth beneath the glorification of vanity.

"To me, it represents the grim pursuit of prestige without the foundation of ability. The social media grist mill rewards grifters, not skilled craftsmen. Kids are choosing e-courses on building their personal brand over trade school. The greatest plumber is nameless," a Professor of Bozonomics read verbatim from the program's brochure, addressing students of the scene who only wanted 'fit pics so that they could stunt on the ugly side-profiles of their clouted betters.

"He's got a point, it may come from a can but it's there," Penny said, speaking not to Jack but to a broad scoffing at the work on display from beneath a pink shawl.

Heels rounded with fresh companionship, they all wound their way to a "cryptic gathering" at a cheap phrontistery, color-coded books with blank pages and self-serve bar in chrome-countertop kitchen. Derpy dudes with white tees poking out from under black hoodies mingled with co-eds paid for their time. A six-foot landscape painting opened into a secret drawing-room for the ceremonies of the anonymous hosts.

"There's always a more exclusive party," Jack said with contempt, speaking not to Penny but to an intense fellow tormenting him with a coke-fueled diatribe about illegal immigrants imported to New York from the porous Texas border.

"You know, I'm essentially a classical liberal, but I think these people need to be rounded up and shot through the jaw."

The next stretch of daylight fast-forwarded across the sky until inky gloom dawned again: two pairs of feet parked outside a mid-century synagogue, smooth curves of concrete suspended above a gated entryway like a machine press, the factory floor a space to discuss signs in the Third House of Venus before checking in for the experimental noise show in the *mikdash* above, hallways to bathrooms and Torah table-talk lounges weighed down with pictorial reminders of that incomplete final solution, the whole building a testament to a task half-finished.

"Their savior came and went. They missed the boat. This is a Godless place," Penny said.

The music kicked off before she got ticked off. The buzzing of insects on the track reminded Jack of southern summers, not because of the cicada canopy polluting the airwaves, but instead due to a handful of similar events popping up near the dumpsters of a Mexican cantina: two or three shmucks, beards either too pronounced or like the fuzz of discarded lollipops, hunched over a MIDI controller, twisting knobs to produce aural rubbish for a crowd of pretenders bobbing their heads.

Strobe lights cleared epileptics from the hippodrome, a wellspring of Talmudic rites filled with revving engines and dynamo hums, an explosion of sonic appropriation from the industrial revolution, machinist innovators behind the decks. After twenty-odd minutes—less time than it had taken for people to struggle through the winding line outside—the headliner absconded to a three-story townhouse uptown to blow down with assorted art hoes and internet bodybuilders. With nothing compelling on the docket, Jack and Penny tagged along, she to acquire connections further up the music-business escalator, he to complete an ethnographic expedition and see if this tangential subculture's afterparty would be any more of a dying duck in a thunderstorm.

Jack squeezed through a door-jamb past a pair of cokeheads with animal nicknames. He spied a news-clipping of the Obama family bowing under a LANDSLIDE VICTORY headline, framed on the wall with an '07 voter registration card and a canted photograph of a Caucasian couple celebrating at the inauguration. Suspended above the mantle, clearly the pride and joy of an empty-nester's living room, was an aspirational sculpture of two young black children in the midst of a skyward leap to dunk on a hoop. Eavesdropped rumors came flooding in.

"I heard there's half a basketball court beneath the apartment's bottom floor."

"The Underground Railroad of Gramercy Park. That explains the lack of African-Americans up here."

On his way to a prosaic mood, Jack sniffed around for his girl, remembering the shindigs of prior eras when he'd find lovers kissing friends after taking wrong turns 'round corners. He spotted Penny, parked on a couch in a menagerie of other zoomers, a young black man leaning a little too far into her bubble. Jack chose the seat between them, a microscopic slice of scarlet cushion, with nary an "excuse me" to smooth his passage.

"Can I have a piece of gum?" the guy asked her, leaning over Jack. She dug around her purse for the pack. "Nah, I want *that* piece," he said, pointing at the one mid-chew in her mouth.

Jack offered his hand for Penny to spit. The guy bounced away to mack on another chicklet. A gal in full Weimar Republic regalia provided a few freebies of nose candy, which Penny declined, so Jack snagged a double dose. The tram home brought renewed attention to their affairs, courtesy of a bitter incel in sheepskin, projecting his insecurities.

"Are you happy? Like really, truly happy," he said to Jack, who could only muster a laugh in return.

"He's not the type to bother with these foolhardy, inward-facing concerns," Penny answered on his behalf.

The stranger mumbled something biting and sunk his head in his hands. Jack escorted Penny to the distant end of the empty car and sparked a bodega pre-roll. A shotgunned exchange of cannabis breath propelled them northward.

Jack's medicinal march against the cough festering inside, plus the passing wish for time on the town sans girlfriend, led him to dial up remote acquaintances for a drink, including an antagonistic short-story scribe named Alexander. The two men had been introduced because of their strikingly similar physiognomy: tall and blonde, a pair of clown princes, which naturally created conflict whenever one of them encroached on the soil of what the other considered his personal kingdom. At an aging punk's Chinatown haunt, they knocked back a bevy of beer-shot combos while Alex explained the premise of his debut novel.

"So there's this black broad all hot and bothered for a man of Irish ancestry. He couldn't care less and fails to give her the time of day, so her brother, a card-carrying gang member, threatens him with grievous bodily harm if he doesn't lay pipe into his sister, so the Mick starts boning the Nigerian princess. A few weeks pass without incident, then a rival gangbanger gets a hard-on to stop this madness and save his sista from the clutches of ol' whitey, coming in hot with his own menace in the Mick's ear. So now the dude is stuck, bound to get his ass hammered either way. It's like Shakespeare but with interracial intrigue. That's all I got so far."

Jack downed another jigger of gin and offered his feedback, trying to parse whether the envy was wrapped up in skin-color or romantic jealousy.

"Not the point. All events are played for comedic ends."

"Ok, then the two hoods should be revealed to be homosexuals, and their unholy union squashes the long-standing beef between communities Gay and African."

Alex laid into Jack for his insolence, repeating key phrases for emphasis, lecturing in a style aped from the preacher's lectern.

"You are one of the more unpleasant fuckers available to hang out with," Jack sniped.

"At least I don't shit the bed as a wingman. Remember last time we met? I totally had that chick in the bag 'til you came up spouting off about Mr. Jones," Alex fired back, citing the period a year prior when Jack quit his antidepressants at the behest of a paranoid client, who later refused to transfer a large sum of capital for services completed, sending the hustler into a black-pilled spiral of internet conspiracy intake.

"Even if she wasn't a couple leagues out of yours, you were too wasted to find the hole, and any hole would do. That explains the flaming subtext of your retarded-ass book."

Alex chuckled, the ominous laugh of a hired foil too serious about the gig work.

"That's rich, considering the circumstances. Do you know where that little minx of a singer-songwriter is right now? I've seen her around, on the arms of older guys. I could tell you exactly how and when she's cheated on you, but I'll spare us both the gooey details. The price of our next round says you won't believe me anyway."

The two men finished their swill in silence.

Simone pinged Jack with an arcane invitation to a "debate society"—coded language spanning the gamut between intimate authorial meet 'n' greet, like last time, and max-capacity interpersonal-chaos barn-burner, also like last time, but later. When the beverages were made to order and paid for by the house, and the guests were political pariahs embroiled in a zero-sum game for crumbs, all heads rolled towards "let them eat cake" debate.

The mid-afternoon April sun illuminated his steps out of the Canal station, a journey from motorized rat banquet to streetside sting operation. Dozens of plainclothes cops arrested hundreds of Somalian entrepreneurs for hawking bootleg purses, carting away the merchandise in stake-bed trucks while the "alleged" perpetrators—as though standing three feet from bogus goods wasn't a strong enough indication of guilt—rode off in extendo paddy wagons.

Back at The Turf for the first event since Amante's book launch, Jack fist-bumped the doorman and pressed the PH button on the elevator panel. After an antique roadshow metamorphosis over the previous few weeks, the waxed and varnished floor supported a row of solid-oak shelves and innumerable pamphlets, manifesto zines, and self-published screeds, an Opposite Day anarchist bookstore, a lending library favoring heterodox viewpoints. There was also a brown chest of drawers masquerading as a makeshift bar.

The room was filled with an overwhelming amount of half-mast males, in dire need of a testosterone booster; not a single woman, married or otherwise, could be seen, save for Simone conspiring in the corner. White wedding chairs were arranged around a battered monitor, displaying the text MEN AGAINST MAGNA CARTA, a bouncing screensaver.

Christ Almighty, maker of Heaven and Earth, the campaign was tiresome from the start. When would that white flag fly? The ends were intangible, the means a mere holding company of shell games, misfits and mystics and bookies shoehorning their searing visions and insidious aims into New York nightlife, hoisting the colors of incompetent ringmasters, Amante then Simone then whoever comes next, women with minimal interior lives, eager to raid the bandwagon and commandeer its reins for their midwit popularity contests. Of course, Jack was pleasant to the two-faced; they might could help him snag a bag or pad his stats.

"Who's up first to moan and groan?"

"It's less a debate"—obviously—"and more of a support group for the disenfranchised, guys afflicted by a jarring loss of God-given privilege due to recent shakedowns of the pecking order. But shhh, we're beginning!" Simone said, enthusiasm showing for this dissident playground she was welding together.

The captain of the club stepped behind the television and spoke into a hidden camera, favoring the homebound watchmen over the seated attendees, his sole visible attributes during the livestreamed speech a pair of stumpy arms gesticulating wildly on either side of the TV, which now scrolled towards oblivion with comments and questions from the digital masses.

Unable to stomach this regal junk-food bumbledom, even when he was compensated for every candy-assed bite, Jack ducked out and phoned a self-taught painter who had expressed interest in a portrait session with the fadingly infamous Magna Chad.

"Drop by my studio uptown," said Craig Stag, real name unknown, failing to mention that his residence was way the hell over in Washington Heights. The A train skipped sixty blocks in seven-league boots, swift as a lamplighter, dropping Jack off at dusk.

Craig rented the spare bedroom of an undignified hoarder, forcing Jack to climb past fifty fraying fur coats and two full editions of the thirteen-volume *Encyclopedia Helvetica* in order to reach the easel and raised stool. From every wall of the studio hung framed impressionistic nudes of Puerto Rican men, real headbreakers, their dark tree-trunk schlongs dangling above Jack's scalp, practically grazing his cream-colored follicles.

Craig plied the younger man with tequila and begged him to maintain his composure, dabbing shades from his palette and carrying on half a conversation. One of those elder statesman gays, Craig claimed that the naked portraits were a fascination distinct from his homosexuality; these fellas were local boxers, and he was proud to be the official sketch-artist of their underground fight club.

He depicted the increasingly-inebriated Jack in Klaus-Kinski-core fresco, emphasizing his Germanic brow and lunatic eyes, a mayoral candidate for Bedlam. Craig paused his brushstrokes to stare hard at Jack, a fusion of dehortation and desire.

"You have a monster inside. I can see it, the canvas reveals all."

Craig continued to illustrate his subject: a maniac, a vampire, externalized characteristics of a tempestuous interior, his guts deemed Godless by this autoerotic arbiter of silhouette. After an hour of stillness, Craig revealed the rough draughtsman's draft, and Jack was shocked to gaze into his corrupted reflection, a dark prince reigning over the nocturne.

"We can finish another day, it takes a few sitdowns to hone in on the essence of a person. I have to jet, tonight is the first springtime fracas of the Bronx Bruisers and I need to capture the combatants in oil. Want to join? I've got a spare ticket if you help me carry in the supplies."

In no position to veto such an effective pitch, Jack followed Craig into the night towards the untrodden territory of that fifth borough, home of the Yankees and much worse. This month's Bronx Bruisers tourney had taken over a mechanic's stone yard, a fighter's playpen constructed from barrels and taut tweed rope, with scrap-cars wheeled in for ringside seats. The two contenders were lightly sparring with coaches and trainers in opposite corners. Hustlers collected bets and explained the odds. Big girls with their bellies out bought buckets of chicken to share with pencil-thin boyfriends, a seed-oil feast of bones and styrofoam for the next morning's custodial staff. A hip-hop air-horn blared, and the dark-skinned titans tapped gloves before wailing on each other with consecutive widowmakers. Craig furiously documented the fight from behind his easel, the smog of virility appearing as a red, blue, and white paste on his canvas, blood and welts and homebrewed piña coladas.

Jack's intrusive ideation escaped the garage, his memories Tokyo-drifting to and fro: a lady wrestler with GMO knockers threatening to impale him on her strap-on if he didn't screw her right; a black chick pounded so hard after splitting an eight-ball that her weave slipped off.

"Can I borrow your smart phone?" Jack asked of a focused Craig, ostensibly to map a route back to Manhattan, the cloud of a catastrophic decision condensing around his fingertips.

Christening the port-o-potty as his personal office, Jack latched the door and unlocked the device, quickly navigating to a harrowing hall of mirrors, thumbnails, unreasonably proportioned women engaging in lewd acts helping him window-shop his way through a relapse in real-time, more babes and broads than could ever be assembled naked in the flesh of meatspace, teens and MILFs and Latinas and BBWs, reward center of the brain hijacked and crashed into towers of primal pleasure, reactivating his old stress-relief pressure valve, the sex magick of semen retention flushed like foul drugs, sacrificing fluids spawning future children to a phantasy of adult-actress code and depositing them in a mound of literal shit, floating back to the thick throes of peak addiction, hunched over the toilet, six feet tall and ejaculating to the image of some poor waif who'd walk into the apartment with a loving smile on her lips minutes later, or spank-calling prior exploits at the witching hour whenever cranked on speed and diabolically horny.

His actual cell rang, shattering the fugue for the shame to seep in. It was Penny. He silenced the pre-loaded tones and waited for the text, which promptly appeared.

Gwen and I are sipping martinis at the French joint where we first broke bread, please join :)

A banging on the flimsy plastic walls of the freestanding stall shook Jack into action. He returned Craig's phone, sans search history, with an apology barely registered by the frantic caricaturist, then escaped on a series of southbound trains. An abuela in a cowprint romper warned of thieves invading their tram; a chilling, slender presence entered the edge of his vision, glitching backwards and grinning through a chrome grill.

Jack pulled up to the corner of 1st and Houston to join Penny and Gwen at their signature spot in the back, embarrassment lurking beneath the mask of his icy demeanor. The girls were discussing some movie, the final opus by a deceased savant, a film that embodied the financial and cultural capital of the world despite being lensed on a London soundstage, its narrative traversing a spread of parties and locations across a single evening, the model for any "damn, I can't believe I'm here of all places at 5am" kind of night.

"It's surprisingly chaste, and pro-marriage to boot," Penny said.

Gwen agreed. "The weirdos who take inspiration from the screen to organize clandestine fuckfests are so far off base they're tickling the moon."

Jack mumbled his endorsement and slumped over in the booth, a star student of delirium tremens. The talk naturally turned to general dispositions towards the sexless and rarified, aloe vera carried down from the mount of past lives to keep the wound green. Her thumb unknowingly on the crimson button, Penny launched the first salvo.

"I can be fickle, sure. In high school I wouldn't let my boyfriend finger me. A couple weeks later I lost my virginity in a trap house, to the big lion of the drug den. First time smoking weed too, a whole night of firsts. I don't remember much."

Jack's blood boiled, platelets burned alive in the inferno of a jealous rage. His perception of injury required reparations, and he would stake his claim to ravage with fire.

"I used to spend nights in the bowels of a house malignant with hoodrats after my frivolous influencer girlfriend shacked up with some stern hip-hop wigga. She got pregnant and stuck him with the disposal receipt. Questionable paternity, could've been me. I'm sure she let his whole crew hit, too. I didn't mind, even though that dumb hoe sold compromising photos of my cock to underwrite our trip to the west coast to crash with a camgirl and a pot dealer. Saved me money in the long run, and the wigga's housemate was a rapping stripper who nearly clawed the skin off my back, her idea of good loving as distraction," Jack slurred, a bitter recall of his encounters with the dregs of Georgia gunshow carnies.

His inability to accept the basic tenets of love, generously given, encouraged a dangerous streak of self-destruction, the never-ending quest for an excuse to watch the world crumble. If all her affection was funded by the CIA, why not turn the screws on agents and handlers to fulfill the prophecy foretold?

Penny responded in kind, sharing intimate details of her flings with musical transvestites and Mexican cokeheads and former sexpats returning from beyond the border. It was easy to forget that she wasn't a virgin.

"I don't think I've ever tapped the Latina market, but that Jamaican chick was a barrel of monkeys," Jack stabbed, unaware of the direction of the knife.

Gwen looked at Penny. "Your ex was too, right?"

Had the restaurant served clichés instead of clams, the moment for a record scratch would have been nigh.

Jack recoiled, visible and visceral. "Your ex was black?"

Penny directed an unsavory look towards her friend.

"He didn't know?" Gwen said, continuing the game of twenty questions.

"More of a caramel color."

His worldview imploded. All those dogwhistles were euthanized by the pound, the country-western nationalist vibes extinguished. The trio finished their lateness-of-the-hour hang. Jack bided his time, plotting verbal revenge from behind the soft-focus veil of his spinning stupor, until Penny sat on the pale-blue bench that would ferry them home.

"I'm not racist, I just didn't think you were the kind of girl to do shit like that."

"I've wasted lots of time on lots of things, and that was two years and a lease and a cat I'll never get back."

"I can't believe it."

"Please don't fixate on this."

"Was he big? Did you enjoy that black dick inside of you?"

"You're being awful. He was a scrawny twig, practically Lebanese."

"Was this the same guy from the bondage experiments?"

"It was never about the sex, there was romance and courtship like any other relationship."

"What's the worst thing you did together?"

"I won't be bullied into answering stupid questions that will only make you feel worse."

"How many men have you been with?"

"Quit hounding me."

"How many? I need to know."

"I don't count them like conquests."

"Everyone has a tally hanging above their heads. Double digits?"

Exasperated and cut down to the quick, she gave a number in the range of ten or eleven.

"But why'd it have to be a black guy?"

Jack berated Penny incessantly during the long journey home, glitching at the discovery of information discordant with his vision of her. His mind raced with reflections on his original serious ex and her dark stories, skipping class to be passed around the laps of the football squad.

The train arrived. Jack stormed off, leaving Penny to brave the night alone, a ten-minute separation that he regretted, but not one that quelled his desire to double down via text message.

Are you alright? I'm worried about you getting raped by a pack of wild animals, but you'd probably like it. Maybe even write a song about it.

4

The Wrong Side of Delk

"You're just another petty charlatan living off the shell game."

— Umberto Eco

Much like how the forests of the Pacific Northwest hid witches stew and stitches too, a maudlin gala of incantations after the lights went out, the thick treeline of Atlanta obscured the city's true identity, an embarrassed teenager on the steps of the chess club.

In a borrowed Cadillac convertible, gunmetal gray, Jack considered his own history of shifting loyalties while symbolic locations appeared through the car's windshield. Convention nerd: a middle-aged woman dressed as a comic book villain had stuck her tongue down his throat outside *that* hotel while her husband gleefully leered. Presumed bisexual: groped and catcalled at *that* club in the center of Queer Mecca, where he had simply been angling to build a bridge, all the greater to grift beneath, instead of serving as bait on the line.

Out the window there, that was the townhouse complex where Jack and five of his friends had crammed into a two-bedroom-plus-office with a balcony overlooking the gate, shouting down the passcode during three-story ragers. Guys and gals had shacked up like square dancers, the duck-duck-goose of cheap mattress companions, 'til their social web was an incestuous mess of overlapping lines and jealous tidings, feeding the starved maw of an endless summer.

Jack remembered tumbling with a tribe of other late-stage teenagers towards the neighborhood pool, after hours, not a camera onsite. He had scandalized his fellow revelers by receiving a novelty underwater blowjob, the mania back then producing a checklist for exhibitionist licking and sucking in a myriad of public spaces, graveyards and backyards and frontyards and yuppie bars. Once, he nearly flipped a RAV4 on the interstate while some death-wish doll gave him dome from the driver's seat, cruise control roadhead from a redhead with rad tattoos inked on pale skin.

Blame the mania again, but he had spent his maturing years floating in and out of BPD pussy. Once that preppy lifeguard party girl had wrapped her spraytanned legs around his torso in the deep end of another pool, promising to open her grandfather's coffers after graduation so he wouldn't have to schlep through a business degree at state uni, he was hooked. There were enough borderline notches carved in his bedpost to whittle a magic wand.

Jack pulled into the driveway of his former home: five subterranean years in a castle of cooze, haunted by a staggering number of physical attachments. He recalled one particular idiot gal, pissed that her pathetic starfucking failed to yield Hollywood mentorship; this was the same phrenology victim who had soaked his comforter while they rounded second or third base, yet demurred before penetration because she needed to solicit her boyfriend's consent. Their first date had fallen to pieces thanks to Jack's observation that her imaginative thesis—"the personal is political"—would probably look better on a bumper sticker.

Jack's joyride through the old and the lewd was cut short by an abrupt tapping on his car window.

"Still pitching a yurt in your shorts on the regular, I see." Jacques Green, The Color of Money, his ex-landlord, spoke with an ethnicized accent as fabricated as his dirty Creole name.

A swarthy ancient practicing voodoo and a bonafide conspiracy theorist, Jacques had a tendency to dominate all conversation with far-fetched claims about his activities at certain key points of cosmic significance during this previous Turning, ever since the second World War had spawned the nation of Zion. Whatever you might think, he had been there too, and yes, it's all true, except for what's not.

Jack had tolerated his subsistence under that incontinent verbal thumb; the rent was free and the presents were generous, even if he couldn't squeeze a word in edgewise—the gift of gab, the curse of chatter. On one occasion, Jack had blacked out from rage while throttling the sagging, scarf-laden neck of a shocked Jacques. They had since cleared the air, an apology traded for a monologue, an admission of guilt exchanged for an anecdote.

Jack sheathed the convertible's key and trailed behind the older man into the overgrown backyard, a forest of bamboo shoots, ladybug-infested leaves and stone statues of Eastern demonology, roll-called from Krishna to Buddha.

"Aiming for a more natural aesthetic?"

"I've thus far failed to acquire reliable help. You were the golden slave," Jacques replied with a wink, the near-dementia fusing with sharecropper sensibilities up top to form a leaky case of confused socio-historical racial identity. In his previous life, the younger man had bought shelter with labor, an arrangement pleasing to his anti-fiat barter-economy elder but of some concern to his traditional family upbringing.

"Who's reliable anymore? Certainly not the bosses," Jack said, digging through a text chain with that bitch Amante for proof.

He showed Jacques a full-autocorrect salvo from his recent master: koans of disappointment over his inability to alchemically transform her raw lumpen coal into entertainment-industry gold, plus a few subtle jabs at his narcissism for developing into an internet personality ahead of her.

"Look at this word choice: *I need more*," Jack said. "Why do women always make that demand? I was all-in on her scheme, to the detriment of my own rising star. And what's there to show for it? Months of income spent like a middle-school moron and a layoff letter delivered via instant message."

Jacques nodded, cataracts scanning over the tiny flip-phone screen, reading the exchange. "I must be frank with you my boy, half of these referential phrases signify nothing. Dox? Longhouse? MAGA Carta? I need an instructional course in scene politics simply to grasp the problem, with a workshop in contemporary babyspeak to interpret her choice of language."

The pair sat around rusty patio furniture, seeking refuge from the scorching midday sun.

"Every app, every artist, every boutique eatery, the names are all Da-Doo this, Bee-Burp that, as if iPad kids are reducing the movements of the tongue to preserve energy for their fingers," Jack said.

He wondered if his high-school hookup still lived in the 'hood, a dulce de leche negrita who threw expert neck because her gangbanger ex had forced her to swallow at gunpoint before homeroom each morning. Jack had once made the mistake of wasting gas on a roundtrip pick-up only to be jumped by her ghetto underage classmates, black knuckles triggering black eyes amid cries of "slam some ass in yo' own grade!"

Jacques returned with a platter of fish sticks and a vial of wormwood absinthe. "Ready to rope me back into our dialogue?"

"When did you depart?"

"Shortly after your chin went slack and your groin went whack."

Jack rubbed his temples. "I've had a tremendously strange couple of days. Did I tell you I took a trip to Memphis with my father?"

Pop and boy had witnessed a crime in progress, three urban crooks onboard a flatbed truck colliding with a soccer mom van, the woman's forehead on a horn that would never stop blowing, the trio scrambling to collect their cash sacks before sprinting in place, ready to accelerate, a cartoonish cloud of cinnamon soul dust accumulating around their ankles, shins, knees, and then THEY WERE OFF! Two slipped under a bridge, one leaped over a fence, and the full police academy dripped sweat in hot, *hot* pursuit, until a well-placed slide-tackle ended the slowest goon's forty-yard dash in a sparse lot.

"It's been a long road since the heyday of Elvis and Orbison, eh?" Jack's father had said.

"I suppose that's why Sun Records operated a few blocks away from the bustling center of Beale," his firstborn son had replied.

They approached the heart of downtown, a legendary African-American cultural district teeming with biker gangs, screeching livestock, and an encroaching land war between Hasidic Jews in full regalia and Black Israelites packing sidearms.

"I Know Why the Caged Chicken Screams," Jack's pa had mused while perusing a rack of wide-brim archeologist head coverings, deciding on a subtle milk-and-cocoa number that fit his cranium with purpose.

Further into their mid-afternoon walkabout, two gentlemen who vaguely resembled the other robber-stooges had accosted the elder Valentine about his purchase.

"I like that hat, man," the squat fellow had said, finger-gun cocked sideways beneath his chin.

"Thank you kindly!" the wearer had announced, without a hint of fear.

"What size it is?"

"My size."

"I said what size is yo' noggin, nigga—"

"Whoa whoa whoa," Jacques interrupted, "you can't just strafe me with an N-bomb like that. Am I intended to slurp up this fantastical story?"

"I'm quoting the crook, he genuinely said 'Noggin Nigga' without cracking a grin. Anyway, we kept our shirts and accessories by stepping into a fried palace for a homestyle lunch. After a pound of meat apiece and as many beers, my dad's bloodthinners doubling the ABV, we dug into the conversational carcass: the women we put up with and why we love them."

Jack shared his lamentations over Penny's copper-colored past, the whiplash of months spent pretending to be rapt little virgins, her dishonesty by omission, his stern-faced sexual filibuster.

"You're going steady with a single gal?"

"Yes, we're together, though after learning of her grim priors in the sack, I'm unsure about the commitment, which I relayed to the receptive audience of my father. He spun a story about his first wife and how the holy vows, sickness or health, swimming in gold or dead-broke, had not prepared him for handling her immense and unsolicited scrutiny of his every activity. What would become her defining personality trait arrived well after the ceremony, and the discovery naturally led to divorce."

Jacques leaned forward, itching to inject a tangent of his own. "Who could survive under such psycho-domestic conditions?"

"It's the Betrothed of Theseus, how much radical emotional change until she is no longer the same gal? I Married A Skinwalker."

With a piercing eye on this opportunity, Jacques launched into an alternate narrative, aiming to obliquely comment on the original topic through self-styled divergent thinking.

"I had lived in Atlanta for over ten years by the time the '96 Olympics rolled into town. The homeless population disappeared, virtually overnight. The mayor's office was caught buying bus tickets in bulk to ship them north, but there were street rumblings of occult explanations, especially concerning those female bums. Ritual orgies in the athlete's encampments, disposal in the dark wooded perimeter 'round the burgeoning town. That was the tail end of the lawless era, my dreams of barbershop quartet stardom were locked away with Wayne, and the succedaneum nightmares were leaking into our day-to-day. On Moreland at dusk I saw fat-assed prostitutes mindlessly following shaggy leviathans while they bounded on all fours into the black."

A chill settled over their low-grade luncheon despite the boiling May afternoon.

"I spun some yarn of my own on the plane ride. May I recite a selection?"

"My story is completely true—"

"I call this one *The Edict of Brain Worms.*" Jack cleared his throat. "In high school, John Valenté served as the de facto leader of an interracial squad of young comedians. He had black friends. He had more than black friends, he had an honorary black card, awarded by a homeless man after learning that John was a casual fan of Isaac Hayes, singer of the theme song for *Shaft.* On stage, the crew's jokes and gags didn't punch up or down, but sideways, in a circle of gentle mockery: John ribbed Jawn (black), Jawn ribbed Yuehan (Chinese), Yuehan ribbed Juan (Spanish), Juan ribbed Jean (French), etc. The humor tickled the audience pink with pleasure, and not one grinning mug ever grew offended. Times were different."

"I can't stand stand-up, the attention whores of the lesser stage with their—"

"Years later, John briefly dated a brick house broad who had recently converted to an esoteric cell of Lutheran Christianity. Not to be crude, but she gave the best head on this side of the Jordan River, expert-level professional-grade deluxe blowjobs, really licked him clean. Unfortunately, she self-flagellated about this well-honed skill, spending time in the confessional booth each Sunday, describing the sexual acts in explicit detail to some poor priest making a tent of his tunic. Double unfortunately, she also indicated several minor tendencies of white supremacy, including romantic flings with Lost Cause true-believers and online patronage of the folk-singin' granddaughters of the national director of the Knights of the Ku Klux Klan, which sounds like a fun romp of a kung-fu film to someone who doesn't know better."

"The woes of repressed desire, my great-aunt Lucille was—"

"The more man-hours and large cash gifts that John invested in his trendy, traditionally-minded girlfriend, the more he realized that her slimy views were merging with, nay, *overtaking*, his moderate liberal sensibilities. When the two of them walked down streets of lower economic status, passing future hip-hop stars and/or crime statistics, John instinctively felt himself throw a protective arm around her bare shoulders to ward off the perceived threat of non-white suitors, who without fail refused to recognize his libidinal ownership and adamantly cat-called in her general direction each and every time."

"There's this pernicious myth about black-on-black—"

"Eventually, John confronted his lover about her odd behavioral responses when the boys on the block flirted in their forceful way. She claimed to be disgusted by the cross-cultural attention, yet often exchanged phone numbers with the men under the pretense of 'collaborating' on 'music' (she was a talented throat singer), while also spending her idle hours 'learning the tongue' of Jamaican patois on social 'language acquisition' applications. John pressed further in pursuit of God's honest truth, asking hard-hitting follow-up questions like, 'Why do you attend church in a bad part of town when your apartment is right next to a beautiful cathedral,' forcing her to reveal a string of one-on-one infidelities and a harrowing gang-bang in a trap house."

"The God Gene strikes again—"

"In a fit of blind rage, John screamed obscenities and punched a wall, taking the Lord's name in vain and bruising his knuckles in the process. He felt betrayed, not just in light of his alleged future wife's rampant whoring, but also because he had grown incrementally more racist over the course of their courtship, largely against his will, only to learn that her bigotry was a bizarre coping mechanism, a false front, mere lip service."

"This character could be considered misogynistic unless—"

"Due to his explosive episode, John's voluptuous broad broke his heart for good by exiting the relationship, citing poor communication as a post hoc justification for her cheating, which she also summarily denied. Left alone, he weighed the option of suicide before deciding to start fresh, by moving to Hollywood to resurrect the Hays Code's moral rules for motion pictures: appropriate language, positive portrayals of family, and avoiding controversial topics such as miscegenation."

"I loved film noir before that period. The pinnacle of the femme fatale."

Jack caught a gander at the coruscated ruby ring on his older friend's pointer, one of eight sporting various stones spread across a pair of wrinkled hands. Jacques held up his two bare digits, imitating the rude gesture salute of a subculture-enforcing punk.

"To your father's point, I respect the sanctity of marriage, despite never tying the knot myself."

Jack nodded curtly in agreement. More than a sabbatical, less than an exile, he flew back to Atlanta as a member of his middle brother's wedding party, the one homecoming king among 'em.

"Can I sniff through your collection of wedding bands? Women's sizes."

The two men strode into the house, a magpie's paradise resupplied by raiding Tutankemen's afterlife deadstock: decorative vases with edible organ meat, funhouse mirrors that changed your pigmentation, and enough precious jewels to operate a power station on Pluto—nominal proof confirming the quodlibet of that movie about a starship cruiser ripping the curtain of the real to unleash an interdimensional feast of torture-sex and entrails: outer space is Hell, literally.

Jacques opened a foam case of female wedding rings and raised an inquisitive eyebrow.

"I think I need to marry my girlfriend. She won't let me hit, in the Biblical sense. I'm flying her down to play my date at little bro's ceremony, and I'd like to make the reception about me by proposing," Jack said.

Jack held up an understated vintage diamond. After half a decade of hard yardwork, he hoped that Jacques might present him with the radiant Macguffin for next to nothing.

"What's this young lady's name and occupation?"

"Penny Delphine. Chanteuse."

Jacques twirled his paws, contemplating the moral and economic ramifications, then plucked a half-used pack of late-Reconstruction stationary from a nearby drawer.

"If you can provide a little context for these prima facie desire lines, the chronicle of your relationship with Lady Delphine thus far, I'll throw you this old gem complimentary."

176

Jacques gathered the flowing folds of his Taiwanese bathrobe and fled the study.

Jack struggled to concentrate, finding countless objects of distraction to draw his gaze, display-case toys and too much noise. Should he address this missive to his missus? His former master? Some mischievous third option? His eyes landed on a micro model of the Unabomber's cabin, and he began scribbling his greeting to a faraway prison penpal.

Dear Professor Kacz...

"The plane doors were inches from closing when this giantess came stomping down the jetway, ranting about discrimination, claiming she needed a full row for her wide ass."

"Did you have to move or something?"

"The entire seating chart was recreated in her image while she blabbed on a video call at max volume about the injustice of it all."

"Well beggars can't exactly moonlight as choosers. I spent some of my final dollars on your ticket." Jack stomped the car's pedal to its metal, speeding northward after a curbside pick-up at the nation's largest layover for sex-trafficking victims.

"Please drive safe, you have precious cargo." Penny lounged with a haphazard enticement, riding shotgun sans seatbelt.

"We need to teleport or I'll miss my brother's rehearsal dinner."

"Better to arrive alive."

"No sense of urgency for the affairs of others."

"You can't seriously try and blame me for stuff outside my control."

"Maybe hop in the car humbly and lead with an apology instead of immediately diving into a story loaded with complaints."

"The heat from you is unbearable, I won't live under the microscope all weekend."

"I'm trying to fish for even mild concern about this situation."

"Jack, you're attacking me because some fat bitch broke the airplane."

"Why are you always so negative?"

"Why is every conversation a chance for a character judgement?"

"Just fucking get your shit together before meeting my parents."

"I was fine 'til you started railing me. And cursing. It doesn't help, and I won't tolerate this dissection for the rest of the weekend." Penny paused. "I'm waiting for you to say something real."

They arrived after the night-before cake had been served, a moody parade of two facing down the blank stares of guests and activating the pent-up chagrin of Jack's mother, who had imbibed her multi-chardonnay minimum before the second course. She hugged Penny, a flinty and mannered embrace. Jack's father strolled over to sign up for the pitiful meet 'n' greet, a second late and a sucker short.

"Thanks for coming, Penny! You have the same name as the bride!"

Jack had neglected to mention this to Penny ahead of time. He never quite bonded with his brother's fiancée, considering her a replaceable grade school sweetheart well into the third, even the fourth year of their relationship, really only remembering her name when encountering it in official capacities. His perma-flux assembly of residencies meant that the formal invitation to Please Save The Date had never supervened.

"Where is the family staying?" Jack asked his parents.

The chapel was located a slim few miles from Jack's childhood home, yet all the locals had decided to lodge in a double-star hotel for the weekend. The insistent concern over a discount code for DUIs trumped his sober brother's naive desire for a bone-dry reception.

Jack's ma answered with a distant look in her eyes. "Even though you didn't RSVP to this important first marriage among my children"—a twisting knife in the schism of his disharmonious life path—"we saved you a spare room. With two beds."

Akin to the killing fields of Kuwait, where a single misplaced step could blow your bottom-half to smithereens, maternal chatter was a minefield littered with the shrapnel of passive-aggressive timebombs, a dirty payload.

"Can I swap for a suite? I brought a date. You recently met her."

Penny prodded Jack's arm. "He doesn't mean that. Thank you so much for having us."

Jack lifted a lone neurotic finger. "She doesn't speak for me. Why two beds? Am I supposed to take a hint here?"

His mother gestured to the side for her son to continue their exchange in private. "I find it inappropriate for you to bring a girl you've briefly dated and expect conjugal privileges." And out came the box, with stick and string to trap the adult kid in the mire of juvenilia.

"Mom, we've shared a bed every night for months, this is ridiculous."

"What's ridiculous is your tone. Pick your battles wisely. This is not one you'll win."

Jack's father hustled over to intervene. "Please don't offend your mother, we all want this weekend to unfold peacefully."

"I'm not responsible for her emotional regulation. I'm twenty-seven years old and will obviously be sleeping next to my girlfriend."

"Sure, next to her, with a yardstick between you," his mother said.

"This is fucking absurd! I'll push the beds together, or we'll cram into one."

Mom's smirk grew ever more chilling. "I've already befriended the hotel's cleaning staff, who will periodically check to ensure both beds are distinctly occupied. Remember what I told you when you were a tiny, insolent firecracker? I have eyes and ears *everywhere*. That's never changed."

Jack fumed and stomped back over to Penny, who offered no comfort or sympathy. He inked a furious thought or two in his private notebook, the epistle-in-progress to Uncle K. growing in breadth, taking on the character of a genuine diary, the unfolding literary saga of his dark romantic—

"What's that you're writing?"

There was a drilling sensation when an abysmal Top 40 hit got stuck, spinning its wheels in the skull; royalty-free streams that suggested the sway of ass-shaking household names, extending beyond their artificially-enhanced abilities in the studio; pure propaganda, the power to hypnotically remind the listener that his behavior needed to change. He must be both more sexual and a greater ally of male feminism, told to gently fuck on command and not to demand a suck and, ideally, to go ahead and tuck, to eradicate the phallus and embrace an estrogenic future: there would be a global matriarchy of sperm donors and sapphic nuclear families in which the muzak in supermarkets, at bowling alleys, and on the sides of scrolling screens would be so psychologically overwhelming that any dream of freedom would find itself trampled by Mephisto's catchy refrains, repeated for sixteen bars in a row.

Jack's vision for Penny's career was an antidote, the sonic saving grace that would rumble over the material world. He told her as much from the bottom of his heart, and a number of cups, swerving around country backroads in a dirt-ditch effort to foil the early whiff of a break-up.

"The only empathy I get from you is an empty promise of the future, which ends up feeling like manipulation tactics," Penny said.

Jack the parrot harped on the same string, a twice-told tale left tasteless after mastication. "I know things suck right now, but I promise we'll get along better soon."

Penny groaned, an ugly guttural sound from the passenger seat, her heart in the possession of a boy who once appeared so intelligent, reduced to a dense block of granite who couldn't emote his escape route out of a brown paper bag.

"We struggle to lift each other out of bad moods, and you lack the wits or charm to make amends."

His brother called and invited Jack and Penny to his fiancée's parents' suburban rental property, where the other age-appropriate bridesmaids and groomsmen were yanking each other's chains while breaking liquid bread. On the car radio was a quiet news bulletin: Ted Kaczynski had died at the age of eighty-one.

Lost among dark lanes, a two-man no-navigation slapstick routine thanks to their respective flip phones, Jack eventually spun a celebratory donut around the cul-de-sac upon recognizing a familiar arrangement of motor vehicles, with rear-window decals lending support to college football squads and ballet bootcamps.

"I'm wiped from the travel, I want to go to the hotel."

"We don't have to stay long."

They slid out of the car and approached the house, entering the time loop of a youth group lock-in, non-alcoholic spritzers and towers of pizza and gossip about graduate school. There wasn't an adult in sight. Everyone present was well over eighteen, save for his youngest brother, in basketball shorts, shooting selfies to three separate freshmen crushes from the corner. And yet, the one-year gap between this clique of live-at-home good-graders and Jack's incel temptress was brazen, self-evident, the rift a natural byproduct of Penny's rough 'n' tumble upbringing and the kill-what-you-eat lifestyle of contemporary New York.

The two stoner bridesmaids beckoned for Jack to follow them behind the back patio to spark a joint. He gladly joined, eager to parse through the writing on the wall with elevated perspective. Penny skipped the sesh and settled into a deck chair to discuss the gift of virginity with the wife-to-be, who was just wrapping up a post-pubescent verbal game.

"Never have I ever taken drugs, had sex, or ridden the bus." Quite the hat trick; it eliminated all remaining players.

Jack's philosophy on relationships was seemingly deduced by working backwards from this silly sleepover activity, a phantom checklist for sour conduct so as to always be the first jackass with a closed fist, maturity imagined from inside a pornbrain.

His fellow potheads were discussing cocaine use. "Oh yeah, it flows freely up north," Jack chimed in, gladly stepping into the role of Cool Older Brother From Outta

Town while keeping one ear obsessively peeled on Penny's small-talk with the rest of the gang.

"In a few weeks I'm off to West Texas, my producer Fenix has an uncle with a ranch and a barn for a studio. We plan to record as much material as possible in the span of a few weeks. Who knows what the summer holds afterwards? I'm feeling LA. Have you ever been?"

Without an apartment waiting for him back in Manhattan, Jack would leap at the opportunity to mingle with cattle and clear the cobwebs from their romance while occupying a bunk-bed, gratis. He slid across the pinewood bench to whisper his proposal in Penny's ear.

"I once had an ex who complained that men would tell her she deserved better, failing to deliver on that declaration. I'm too smart to fall into the same trap, so I'll lead with the fact that we deserve each other. We're from the same tribe and must preserve the bloodline. My practical skills can supplement and elevate your unrefined creativity. Once I nab a bag, I can fund your recording and touring until sales and sponsorship deals pay for our house filled with kiddos. I believe in the occasional necessity of divorce but I would never do that to you as long as our personalities stay true."

He gagged on the feet in his mouth. The young lady smokers were busted by the bride's straight-edge father. Penny helped him avoid the other elephant.

"Why do you love me?"

Jack struggled to circumvent the naval blockade surrounding his brain instead of speaking from the heart. He bought himself extra minutes by encouraging the continued discussion from the comfort of their hotel room, not realizing that greater delay established higher expectations of profundity. He gripped the steering wheel in a vise, a sailor in a storm.

"I love you because you're the closest living comparison to a good friend of mine, we never dated, she's like my sister, but her immense passion for life in an era of bored clout princesses make her the archetypal woman in my view, a twenty-first century Eve, or Mary. You two have tons in common, I wish we could all hang, but she's out of town."

Satisfied with his point, if shaky on its delivery, Jack lifted his two o'clock hand off the steering wheel and placed it on Penny's bare, luscious thigh, unable to catch her dour, downtrodden expression with his eyes glued to the road.

"I'm so excited we get to go to the Lonestar state together," he added, breath hot with recycled booze. He parked the borrowed convertible in the barren lot.

Up in their shared room, Jack attempted a sixty-nine style face-fuck before knocking unconscious.

Classy way to describe the supposed "mother of your future kiddos"—gross!

Misuse of my own life and language is parasitic, and this is the evidence!

Write this away as art, but this is not art and clearly defines the distorted way you see me, our life, and relationships in general. I'm a free speech absolutist, but out of care and NOT retaliation. This writing is abhorrent. Not in a provocative way, but in a "you wouldn't want to hear a middle school boy's inner dialogue" way. Not disappointed but repulsed. I didn't expect much more. I hope you find your gift, truly. It's time to reexamine your path, and I pray you have one, because God could not be that cruel.

On another note: it's time to discuss how we are moving forward in a mature way. No more lying to yourself that this is working, that there's a future in this relationship when you choose to demolish it. There is no way to trust someone who doesn't care how low he goes. When something hurts in this way, it is because truth has been experienced. I've seen the truth in your words, how you view me, and I see the truth of how you operate. I have been untruthful in not facing my fears in navigating my life alone and this false way of living has been repeatedly revealed to me as a living nightmare.

I do not like how you see the world. I do not want to be of one mind with you, nor a twisted figment of your own. I feel I have regressed back into this state with you out of sympathy, but sympathy does not garner respect. I do not respect your brutish and hard-headed nature. We are called to be reflections of Truth to each other, but I do not feel we are on this same pursuit together. I want peace and revelation for you and it is not in this repetitive state. I wanted to travel there with you in a pure way, truly, but while we bind each other this is just a mirage.

Despite your revisions of me, I am a sensitive soul and I have been through a lot in my life. When your feelings are free to atomically explode, I feel like my life is struck down again and I'm a child without agency, back to where I began, having not learned or grown into the woman I am. Where is the supposed love you have for that girl? What are the consequences for you other than more self-obsession disguised as self-loathing?

I need a protector if I'm to be with anyone at all. Not someone willing to cause complete destruction because their emotions are more true than Truth itself. I am unsure what the way forward looks like for you, but I am sure that it is without me.

May God Bless You,

Penny

www.ingramcontent.com/pod-product-compliance
Lightning Source LLC
Chambersburg PA
CBHW061309210726
48293CB00003B/1183